This whole thing was ridiculous.

Finn had been matched with a woman who'd caused his family immeasurable misery and created a scandal that had spawned countless aftereffects.

The smartest move would have been to turn around and leave without a backward glance. *This* was the surest method to end up insane by the end of the night.

He'd only asked Juliet to dance because manners had been bred into him since birth. This was a party. It was only polite.

But now he wasn't so sure that was the only reason.

Seeing Juliet again had kicked up a push-pull of emotions he'd have sworn were buried. Not the least of which was the intense desire to have her head on a platter. After he had her body in his bed.

* * *

Matched to a Prince is part of the
Happily Ever After, Inc. trilogy.
Their business is makeovers and matchmaking,
but love doesn't always go according to plan!

* * *

If you're on Twitter,
tell us what you think of Harlequin Desire!
#harlequindesire

Dear Reader,

If you've read *Matched to a Billionaire*—or almost any of my books—you know how much I love a good Cinderella retelling. You hold in your hands the most twisted version yet.

Confession time! I'm fascinated by England's Prince Harry. He's charming and clearly loves his family and country, yet he gets into trouble often. I *had* to write my own story of what might drive a prince to star in frequent scandals. A broken heart is the answer, and who better to help our prince move on than a bride selected for him by a matchmaker? Except Prince Alain's matchmaker doubles as a fairy godmother and she plans to reunite him with Juliet, the woman who broke his heart. Along with a king determined to stop his son's scandal-inducing behavior and remnants of the betrayal that tore apart Prince Alain and Juliet, this is a modern-day fairy tale about what happens before the prince and his Cinderella arrive at the ball.

Matched to a Prince is the second title in the Happily Ever After, Inc. trilogy. I've had so much fun writing this series of connected books and if you enjoy Prince Alain and Juliet's story, I hope you'll read the other two! I would love to hear from you. Drop me a note at http://katcantrell.com.

Thanks for reading!

Kat Cantrell

MATCHED TO
A PRINCE

KAT CANTRELL

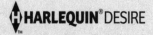

Recycling programs
for this product may
not exist in your area.

ISBN-13: 978-0-373-73334-7

MATCHED TO A PRINCE

Printed in U.S.A.

KAT CANTRELL

read her first Harlequin novel in third grade and has been
scribbling in notebooks since she learned to spell. What else
would she write but romance? She majored in literature, officially with the intent to teach, but somehow ended up buried in middle management in corporate America, until she
became a stay-at-home mom and full-time writer.

Kat, her husband and their two boys live in north Texas.
When she's not writing about characters on the journey
to happily-ever-after, she can be found at a soccer game,
watching the TV show *Friends* or listening to '80s music.

Kat was the 2011 Harlequin So You Think You Can Write win-
ner and a 2012 RWA Golden Heart finalist for best unpub-
lished series contemporary manuscript.

To Cynthia, because this book was so hard to write
and you were there for me every step of the way.
And because TPFKAD had to be in it somewhere.

One

When the sun hit the three-quarter mark in the western sky, Finn aimed the helicopter for shore. It was nearing the end of his shift and, as always, he couldn't resist dipping low enough to let the powerful downdraft ripple the Mediterranean's deep blue surface.

A heron swooped up and away from the turbulence as fast as its wings could carry it, gliding along the air currents with sheer poetic grace. Finn would never get tired of the view from his cockpit, never grow weary of protecting the shoreline of the small country he called home.

Once he'd touched down on the X marking the spot for his helicopter, Finn cut power to the rotor and vaulted from the cockpit before the Dauphin blades had come to a full stop. His father's solemn-faced driver stood on the tarmac a short distance away and Finn didn't need any further clues to recognize a royal summons.

"Come to critique my landing, James?" Finn asked with

a grin. Not likely. No one flew helicopters with more precision and grace than he did.

"Prince Alain." James inclined his head in deference, then delivered his message. "Your father wishes to speak with you. I'm to drive."

Checking his eye roll over James's insistence on formality, Finn nodded. "Do I have time to change?"

It wouldn't be the first time Finn had appeared before the king in his Delamer Coast Guard uniform, but he'd been in it for ten hours and the legs were still damp from a meet-up with the Mediterranean while rescuing a swimmer who'd misjudged the distance to shore.

Every day Finn protected his father's people while flying over a breathtaking panorama of sparkling sea, distant mountains and the rocky islands just offshore. He loved his job, and spending a few hours encased in wet cloth was a small price to pay.

But that didn't mean he wanted to pay that price while on the receiving end of a royal lecture.

James motioned to the car. "I think it would be best if you came immediately."

The summons wasn't unexpected. It was either about a certain photograph portraying Finn doing Jägermeister shots off a gorgeous blonde's bare stomach or about the corruption charges recently brought up against a couple of his running buddies.

A blogger had once joked that Finn's official title should be Prince Alain Phineas of Montagne, House of Scandal. It wasn't so funny to the king, who had tried to combat the negative press with a royal announcement proclaiming Finn's upcoming marriage. A desperate ploy to get his son to settle down.

Hadn't worked so far. Perhaps if his father could actually name a bride, the ploy might get some traction.

Finn paused. Maybe his father had picked someone.

He hoped not. The longer he could put off the inevitable, the better.

But his life was never his own and whatever his father wanted, Finn would deal with it, like always.

Only one way to find out if he'd be announcing the name of his bride soon.

Finn allowed James to show him into the backseat of the town car his father used to fetch people and tried to swallow his dread. The Delamer Coast Guard administrative building disappeared behind them and Finn's homeland unrolled through the windows.

Tourist season had officially started. Bright vendor booths lined the waterfront, selling everything from outrageously priced sunscreen to caricatures quickly drawn by sidewalk artists. Hand-holding couples wandered along the boardwalk and young mothers pushed strollers in the treed park across from the public beach.

There wasn't a more beautiful place on earth, and Finn thanked God every day for the privilege of not only living here but the opportunity to serve its people. It was his duty, and he did it gladly.

Too soon, the car drove through the majestic wrought iron gates of the palace where Finn had grown up, and then moved out of as soon as his mother would allow it. He'd realized early on he was just in the way. The palace was the home of the king and queen, and eventually would house the crown prince and princess, Alexander and his wife, Portia.

Finn was so far down the line of succession, he couldn't even see the head. It didn't bother him. Most days.

A slew of workers scurried about the hundred acres of property surrounding the stately drive. Each employee focused on maintaining the famous four-tiered landscaping that ringed the central fountain bearing a statue of King Etienne the First, who had led Delamer's secession from France two centuries ago.

Another solemn-faced servant led Finn to the office his father used for nonstate business. That was a relief. There'd be no formality then, and Finn could do without royal addresses and protocol any day.

When Finn entered, the king glanced up from paperwork strewn across his four-hundred-year-old desk, which had been a gift from a former president of the United States. Finn preferred gifts you could drink, especially if they came with a cork.

With a small smile, his father pushed his chair back and stood, gesturing to the brocade couch. "Thanks for coming, son. Apologies for the short notice."

"No problem. I didn't have any plans. What's up?"

Since he didn't mistake his father's gesture for a suggestion, Finn perched on the fancy couch at a right angle to the desk.

King Laurent crossed his arms and leaned on the edge of his desk, facing Finn. "We need to move forward with finding you a wife."

Called it in one.

Finn shifted against the stiff couch cushions, determined to find a comfortable spot. "I said I'd be happy with whomever you picked."

A lie. He'd tolerate whomever his father picked.

If Finn and his bride ended up friends as his parents had, great. But it was a lot to ask in an arranged marriage. It wasn't as though Finn could hold out for love, not when it hadn't worked out the one and only time he'd allowed himself to care about a woman.

Juliet's face, framed by her silky light brown hair, swam into his mind's eye and he swallowed. A hundred blondes with a hundred shot glasses couldn't erase the memory of the woman who'd betrayed him in the most public and humiliating way possible. He knew. He'd tried.

"Be that as it may," the king said, "an option I hadn't considered has come to my attention. A matchmaker."

"A what?"

"An American matchmaker contacted me through my secretary. She asked for a chance to earn our business by doing a trial match. If you don't like the results, she won't charge us."

Finn smelled something fishy, and if there was anything he knew after spending the majority of his day in or near the sea, it was fish. "I'm reasonably certain we can afford her fee regardless. Why would you consider this?"

Was this another ploy to get him under his father's thumb? Had the king paid this matchmaker to orchestrate a match with a woman loyal to the crown, who could be easily controlled?

"This matchmaker introduced Stafford Walker to his wife. I've done enough business with him to know his recommendation is solid. If the woman hadn't mentioned his name, I wouldn't have given her idea a moment's consideration." His father sighed and rubbed the spot between his eyes wearily. "Son, I want you to be happy. I liked what she had to say about her selection process. You need someone specific, who will negate all the bad press. She promises to match you with the perfect woman to become your princess. It seemed like a fair deal."

Guilt relaxed Finn's rigid shoulders. "I'm sorry. You've been more than patient with me. I wish…"

He'd been about to say he wished he knew why he courted so much trouble. But the reason wasn't a mystery. She had eyes the color of fresh grass, glowing skin and a stubborn streak wider than the palace gates.

Perhaps this matchmaker might find someone who could replace Juliet in his heart. It could happen.

"I've had this matchmaker, Elise Arundel, thoroughly checked out, but do your own research. If you don't like the idea, don't do it. But I've had little luck coming up with a potential bride on my own." The king smiled, looking like his usual cheerful self for the first time since Finn had entered the room. "There's no shortage of candidates. Just the lack of one who can handle you."

Finn grinned back. "At least we agree on that."

Because Finn took after his father. They both had big hearts and even bigger personalities. And the absolute sense of duty that came part and parcel with being royalty. They shared a love for Delamer and a love for the people they served.

His father managed to do it with grace and propriety. Finn, on the other hand, tended to whoop it up, and photographers loved to capture it. Of course, a photo could never depict the broken heart that drove him to search for a method, any method, to erase the pain.

He got all that and didn't mind the idea of getting married, especially to save himself from a downward media spiral. Finding a woman he could love at the same time was an attractive bonus. Settling down and having babies appealed to him if he could do it with someone who gave him what he desperately wanted—a sheltered place all his own where he could be a man and not a prince, if only for a few hours.

The odds of a matchmaker pulling a name out of thin air who could do that…well, he'd do better betting a thousand on red and letting it ride.

"I'll talk to Ms. Arundel." Finn owed it to his father to figure out a way to stop causing him grief, and he owed it to his country to portray the House of Couronne positively in the international press. If it meant marrying the matchmaker's choice and making the best of it, so be it.

Relief filled the king's eyes and a double dose of guilt swam through Finn's stomach. His father loved him and wanted the best for him. Why couldn't Finn do the right thing as his brother always did? Alexander would be king one day and constantly kept that forefront in his mind. His behavior was above reproach and *he* never caused their parents a moment's worry.

Finn, on the other hand, was the spare heir. Unnecessary. The Party Prince.

An advantageous marriage was a chance for Finn to do something right for once, something of value to the crown. He'd hoped to keep putting it off. But clearly his father was having none of that.

"She'd like you to fly to Dallas, Texas, to meet in person," the king said. "As soon as possible."

Dallas. He'd never been there. Maybe he could pick up an authentic cowboy hat if nothing else.

Mentally, Finn rearranged his calendar for the weekend. He'd committed to attending a couple of charity fund-raisers and had planned to hit a new club in Saint Tropez Saturday night. Looked as if he'd be skipping all of it.

"I've got a shift tomorrow, but I can go the day after."

His father put a gentle hand on Finn's shoulder. "I think it's a good choice."

Ducking his head, Finn shrugged. "We'll see. What's the worst that can happen?"

As soon as the words left his mouth, he regretted them. Scandal followed him like a mongrel dog he'd fed once and couldn't get rid of. Juliet's betrayal had been the first scandal but certainly not the last. It had just hurt the most.

And that was the kicker. She'd hurt him so badly because he'd loved her so much, only to find she didn't feel the same way. If she had loved him, she'd never have participated in a protest against everything he held dear—his father, the military, the very fabric of the governing structure that he'd sworn allegiance to.

The irony. Two things he'd loved about Juliet were her passion and commitment to her family. Without them, she'd be uninteresting and lackluster. Without them, the protest wouldn't have happened.

It didn't matter. She'd killed all his feelings for her. Except the anger. That, he still had plenty of.

Grimly, he bid his father goodbye and let James drive

him back to his Aventador still parked at the coast guard headquarters. His entire life could be summed up in one phrase—dual-edged sword. No matter which way it was wielded, he'd be cut. He would be a man and a prince until the day he died, and it seemed fated that he could never satisfy both sides simultaneously.

Yet he held on to a slim thread of hope this matchmaker might change things for him.

Juliet Villere did not understand the American fascination with small talk. It was boring.

The packed ballroom wasn't her preferred scene anyway, but coupled with a strong desire to avoid one more conversation about the ridiculous game confused Americans called football, the wall had become her friend. It warmed her bare back nicely and provided a great shield from the eyes she'd felt burning into her exposed flesh.

Why hadn't someone told her that a makeover didn't magically transform your insides? All the makeup and fancy clothes in the world couldn't convert Juliet into someone who liked lipstick. Or parties.

But she owed Elise Arundel and her matchmaking-slash-makeover services a huge debt for taking her in when she'd fled Delamer in search of some magic to heal the continual pain of Finn's betrayal. That was the only reason she'd agreed to attend this glittery event full of Elise's clients.

Maybe Elise wouldn't notice if Juliet ducked out the side entrance and walked back to the matchmaker's house in the Dallas district called Uptown, where Juliet was staying until Elise found her an American husband. It was only a couple of miles, and she'd practiced walking in these horribly uncomfortable heels enough times that her leg muscles were used to the strain.

Then she caught sight of Elise heading in Juliet's direction, a determined look on her mentor's face.

Too late.

"Having a good time?" Elise asked, her dark page boy swinging in time to the upbeat song floating above the crowd.

"Fantastic."

The sarcasm clearly wasn't lost on Elise, who smiled. "It's good for you to be in social settings, dressed to kill. I invited you to this mixer so you could practice mingling. Hugging the wall won't accomplish that."

The reminder tightened Juliet's stomach, and she resituated the waistline of the form-fitting green dress her new friend Dannie Reynolds had helped select.

"I have nothing good to say about football." One thing was clear—the American husband she'd asked Elise to match her with would watch it. Therefore, Juliet would likely become well versed in the fine art of faking interest. "So I'm acquainting myself with the benefits of solitude."

Elise laughed. "Dance with someone. Then you don't have to talk."

Juliet shook her head. She'd never danced with anyone other than Finn, and she didn't want to break that streak tonight.

Finn.

Pain, sharp and swift, cramped her stomach. Crossing the Atlantic hadn't dimmed his hold over her one bit.

He'd shredded her soul over a year ago. Shouldn't she be finished healing by now? She wanted desperately to get to that place where he was just some guy she used to date, one she recalled fondly yet distantly.

But the announcement of his upcoming engagement had cut deeply enough to drive her from Delamer all the way to Dallas, Texas. Thank God she'd stumbled over that EA International ad in the back of a fashion magazine she'd thumbed through at the dentist's office back home—it had given her a place to go.

"I don't see the point in dancing with one of these guys."

As she didn't see the point in having fake nails or painted

lips. But it wasn't her place to argue with the formula Elise used in her matchmaking service.

"None of them will be my match," she continued. "And besides, they've all got sports on the brain. Does scoring more points feed hungry children? Right any wrongs? No. It's stupid."

Juliet started to make a face and remembered she couldn't do that anymore. Actually, she wasn't supposed to be so outspoken either. Her American husband would want a refined wife with the ability to mingle with the upper crust. Not a woman who had little use for propriety and fluff. Or the Dallas Cowboys.

How in the world was she going to pretend *that* much for the rest of her life?

The same way she was going to pretend her heart hadn't broken when she'd lost the man she'd loved, her sweet little brother and her life in Delamer.

Anything was manageable if it matched her with a husband who could keep her in the States, and save her from having to watch Finn marry someone else.

With a laugh, Elise shook her head. "No, no. Don't hold back. Tell me how you really feel. How about if I save you from further suspense and tell you I have your match?"

Juliet's heart stuttered to a stop. This was it. The reason she'd come to America.

What would her future husband be like? Did he enjoy swimming and sailing and could she ask him to take her on trips to the beach? Would he be okay with her family coming to visit occasionally? Did he have a nice smile and laugh a lot?

Most important, would she be able to develop feelings for him that would fill the Finn-shaped hole inside?

Even though Elise guaranteed a love match, replacing Finn was probably too much to hope for.

Contentment would be enough. It had to be.

She swallowed the sudden burn in her throat. "That didn't take long. I only finished your questions yesterday."

Shrugging, Elise turned to face the ballroom, her shoulder bumping Juliet's companionably. "Sometimes when I load the profile, I don't get a match against someone already in the system and then we have to wait until new clients are entered. Yours came back immediately."

Juliet wanted to ask for the name. And at the same time, she wanted to dive under the buffet table.

What was she doing here? This man in Elise's system expected a certain kind of woman, one who could host his parties and mingle with his friends, smiling through boring stories of business mergers and tax breaks. And football. That was so not her.

She wanted to go home.

Then she thought about living in Delamer day in and day out and how often she saw Finn's helicopter beating through the broad blue sky. Or how she'd stumbled over another photograph of him cutting the ribbon at the new primary school—that picture would never die.

A little girl who would attend the school had sneaked up and wrapped her arms around his thigh just before he cut the ribbon. Finn leaned down to kiss her cheek and presto. Instant immortalization via the hundreds of camera phones and paparazzi lenses in the audience.

The pictorial reminder of the prince's sweet and charming nature stabbed her in the stomach every time. He was such a good guy, with a sense of honor she'd once loved—until realizing it was a front for his stubborn refusal to see how much he'd hurt her by taking his father's side. There was no reasoning with Finn, and that trumped all his good qualities.

In Delamer, there were constant reminders of the void her brother Bernard's death had created.

Any husband was better than that.

"What happens if I don't like the man your computer

picked?" Juliet asked, though surely Elise's system had captured her exact specifications.

"There are no absolutes. If you don't like him, we'll find someone else, though it might take a while. However..." Elise hesitated. "I'd like you to keep an open mind about the possibilities. This man is perfect for you. I've never seen two more compatible people. Not even Leo and Dannie were this closely aligned, and look how well that turned out."

Juliet nodded. Dannie and Leo Reynolds were definitely one of the most in-love couples in the history of time and had never even met each other before they signed on with EA International and got married. If Elise said this man was Juliet's perfect match, why doubt it?

"I had an ulterior motive for inviting you to the party tonight," Elise confessed. "Your match will be here too. Soon. I thought it would take some pressure off if you met socially."

Her match. Already.

Juliet had hoped for some time to learn more about him before being thrown at his feet. She touched her pinned-up hair. At least she'd meet her future husband while looking the absolute best she could, a small victory in her mind.

Deep breath. Bernard would want her to be happy, to move on. The memory of her brother's smile bolstered her.

A disturbance in the crowd caught Juliet's attention. People craned their necks to peer over each other, whispering and nodding toward the ballroom entrance.

"What's going on?" she asked.

Elise uttered a very unladylike word.

"I was hoping for a little more time to explain. It's your match." Elise cleared her throat. "He's early. I think that's a good quality in a man. I mean, along with all of his other ones. Don't you think so?"

Her future husband, assuming everything went according to plan, had just walked into the ballroom.

Juliet's pulse took off, throbbing below her ears. "Sure. But why does it sound like you're trying to talk me into it? Does he have two heads or something?"

"I did something a little unorthodox to find your match." Elise bit her lip and put her hand on Juliet's arm. "Something I hope you'll appreciate. It was a test. I figured if the computer didn't match you, I wouldn't say anything. I'd never tell you and I'd find someone else for you both."

"What are you talking about? What did you do?"

Elise smiled weakly as the crowd pressed closer to the entrance, blocking their view of whoever had drawn so much interest. "You talked so much about him. I heard what was still in your heart. I couldn't call myself a matchmaker if I didn't give you an opportunity to rediscover why you fell in love in the first place."

The first wave of unease rolled through Juliet's stomach. "Talked about whom?"

"Prince Alain. Finn." Elise nodded toward the crush surrounding the entrance. "He's your match."

"Oh, my God. Elise!" Juliet wrapped her arms around her waist but couldn't stop the flood inside of…everything. Hope. Disbelief. The unquenchable anger at his inability to side with her. "You contacted Finn? And didn't tell me? Oh, my God."

Finn was here. In the ballroom.

He was her match.

Not a quiet American businessman who watched football and would save her from the heartache Finn had caused.

"Open mind," Elise reminded her and grasped Juliet's hand to propel her forward, parting the crowd easily despite being half a head shorter than everyone else. "Come say hello. Give me ten minutes. Let me explain to you both what I did and then you can blast me for my tactics. Or spend a little while reacquainting yourselves. Maybe give it a chance. It's your choice."

Greedily, Juliet's gaze swept the crowd, searching for a

familiar face. And found a solid figure in black tie, flanked by a discreet security team, moving toward her.

Finn. Exactly as her heart remembered him.

Tall, gorgeous, self-assured. Every bit a man who could support the weight of a crown despite the probability that he never would. Hard, defined muscles lay under a tuxedo that did little to disguise the beauty of the man's body. His short, dark hair that had a tendency to curl when he let it grow was the same. As was the winsome smile.

Until he paused in front of Elise and caught sight of Juliet. The smile slipped a touch as his gaze cut between the two women. "Ms. Arundel. It's nice to see you again."

Finn extended his hand and took Elise's, drawing her forward to buss her cheek as if they were old friends. To Juliet, he simply said, "Ms. Villere. What a pleasant surprise. I wasn't aware you were on this side of the world."

In spite of the frost in his tone, his voice flipped her stomach, as it always had. More so because it had been so long since she'd heard someone speak with the cadence intrinsic to people from Delamer.

"The surprise is mutual," she assured him, shocked her throat hadn't gone the way of her lungs, which seemed to be broken. She couldn't breathe. The ballroom's walls contracted, stealing what air remained in the room. "Though I'm reserving judgment on whether it's pleasant."

Stupid mouth had gotten away from her again. The laser-sharp eyes of the crowd branded her back and she became aware of exactly how many people were witnessing this public meeting between Prince Alain and a woman they no doubt vaguely recognized. Wouldn't take long to do an internet search and find videos, pictures and news reports of the scandal. It had garnered a ton of press.

His expression darkened. "Be sure to inform me when you decide. If you'll excuse me, I have business with Ms. Arundel which is not of your concern."

Finn was in rare His-Royal-Highness mode. She hated it when he got that way.

"Actually," Elise corrected with a nervous laugh and held a palm out, "Juliet is your match."

Two

"What?" Finn zeroed in on Juliet, piercing her with steely blue eyes she remembered all too well. "Is this your idea of a joke? Did you beg Elise to contact me?"

Is *that* what he thought? Her brother was dead and afterward, Finn had abandoned her when she'd needed him most. Juliet would never forgive him. Why would she extend one small finger to see him again?

"I had nothing to do with this!" Hands on her hips, she waded straight into the rising tension, eyes and ears around them forgotten as the emotions Finn elicited zigzagged through her torso. "I thought you were getting married. What happened to your princess? What are you doing signing on with a matchmaker?"

A muscle ticked in Finn's forehead. "My father does want me to get married, as soon as I find a bride. That's what I'm doing here. I was promised the perfect match. Amusing how that worked out."

Finn wasn't engaged? There wasn't even a potential

princess on the horizon? She'd left Delamer based on something that *wasn't even true*.

"Yeah, hilarious. I was promised the same."

In tandem, they turned to Elise. She smiled and escorted them both to an unpopulated corner, likely so the coming bloodbath wouldn't spatter her guests. Finn's muscled companions followed and melted into the background.

"Do you remember the profile question about love?" Elise tucked her hair behind one ear with a let's-get-down-to-business swipe. "I asked you both what you'd be willing to give up in order to have it. Juliet, what did you say?"

Arms crossed, Juliet glared at Elise and repeated the answer. "You shouldn't have to give up anything for love. It should be effortless or else it's not real love."

No compromise. Why should she have to completely rearrange her entire belief system to appease one very stubborn man? The right man for her should recognize that she'd tried to upset the status quo only because she'd been forced to.

The right man for her would know he'd been everything to her.

"Finn?" Elise prompted and he sighed.

His gaze softened and he spoke directly to Juliet. "You shouldn't have to give up anything. Love should be easy and natural, like breathing. No one asks you to give up breathing so your heart can beat."

He had. He wanted her to forget Bernard had died serving the king's ego, wearing the same uniform Finn put on every day. She slammed her lids closed and shoved that thought away. It was too much.

"Right. Easy and natural. That part of us wasn't hard."

And with the words, the good and amazing and breath-stealing aspects of her relationship with Finn lit up the darkness inside her.

Everything had been effortless between them. If Bernard

hadn't had that accident, she and Finn would probably be married by now and living happily ever after.

"No. Not hard at all." Finn shook his head, his eyes still on her, searching for something that looked a lot like what she constantly wished for—a way to go back in time.

Which was impossible and the reason she'd fled to the States.

But she'd left Delamer because she thought Finn was marrying someone else. If that wasn't true, what else might she need to reexamine?

Elise put her hands out, placing them gently on their arms, connecting them. "Do you remember what you each said you were looking for in a relationship?"

"The calm in the storm," Juliet said, and her ire drained away to be replaced by the tiniest bit of hope.

"A place where I could just be, without all the other pressures of life," Finn said, his voice a little raspy. "That's how I answered the question."

He didn't move, but he felt closer. As if she could reach out and touch him, which she desperately wanted to do. Curled fingers dug into her thigh. Her heart tripped. This was not a good idea.

"So? We answered a couple of questions the same way. That's no surprise."

Finn agreed with a nod. "I would have been surprised if we didn't respond in a similar vein."

They'd always been of one mind, two hearts beating as one. When they sailed together, they never even had to talk, working in perfect tandem to reef the main or hull trim. They'd met while sailing with mutual friends, then fallen in love as the two of them skimmed the water again and again in Finn's boat.

"So," Elise said brightly, "maybe the better question is whether you can forget about the past and see how you both might have changed. You're in America. The divide you had in Delamer doesn't matter here. It's safe. Take some time on neutral ground to explore whether that effortless love still exists."

That was totally unnecessary. She'd never fallen out of love with Finn and being here in his presence after a long, cold year apart solidified the fact that she probably never would.

But that didn't mean they belonged together.

"Are you a relationship counselor or a matchmaker?" Juliet asked Elise without a trace of guile.

"Both. Whatever it takes to help people find happiness."

Happiness. That hadn't been on her list when she came to Elise, broken and desperate for a solution to end her pain. But instead of an American husband, she'd been handed an opportunity for a second chance with Finn.

He was the only man on earth who could rightly be called her match. The only man she'd ever wanted to let into her heart. That had always been true and Elise had somehow figured that out.

That was some computer program Elise used. Juliet had hoped for a bit of magic. Perhaps she'd gotten her wish.

"Elise is right," Finn said quietly. "This is neutral ground, with no room for politics. And it's a party. Dance with me."

Juliet nodded and hoped agreeing wasn't the stupidest thing she'd ever done.

Elise slipped away, not even trying to hide the relief plastered all over her face.

Juliet's eyelids pricked with tears as something shuddery and optimistic filled her empty soul. She would wallow in her few precious hours with Finn, and maybe it would lead to more. Maybe time and distance had diluted their differences.

Maybe he'd finally understand what his support and strength meant to her. She'd lost so much more than a brother a year ago. She'd also lost the love of her life.

* * *

Finn led Juliet to the dance floor, a minor miracle since his knees had gone numb.

This whole thing was ridiculous. He'd known there was something off about a matchmaker approaching his father, but he never could have predicted Elise's actual motivation or the result of his trip to Dallas.

What would the king say when he realized what he'd inadvertently done? Finn had been matched with a woman who'd caused his family immeasurable misery and created a scandal that had spawned countless aftereffects.

Yet Finn and Juliet had met again, paired by a supposedly infallible computer program. Everybody he'd talked to raved about EA International's process. Raved about Elise and how much she truly cared about the people she helped. So yesterday, Finn had walked through Elise's extensive match profile, answered her questions as honestly as he could and hoped for the best.

Only to have Juliet dropped back into his life with no warning.

The smartest move would have been to turn around and leave without a backward glance. Staying was the surest method to end up insane by the end of the night.

He'd asked Juliet to dance only because manners had been bred into him since birth. This was Elise's party and they were business associates. It was only polite.

But now he wasn't so sure that was the only reason.

Seeing Juliet again had kicked up a push-pull of emotions he'd have sworn were buried. Not the least of which was the intense desire to have her head on a platter. After he had her body in his bed.

Fitting Juliet into his arms, they swayed together to the music. It took mere moments to find the rhythm they'd always shared. He stared down into her familiar face, into the green eyes he'd never forgotten, and felt something loosen inside.

It was *Juliet,* but in capital, sparkling letters with giant exclamation points.

She'd been transformed.

The alterations were external, and he'd liked her exactly the way she'd looked the last time he'd seen her. But what if more than her hair had changed?

Could he really fly back to Delamer without taking a few hours to find out what might be possible that hadn't been possible before?

Now that he had her in his arms, the anger he'd carried with him for the past year was hard to hang on to.

"You look different," he blurted out. *Smooth.* Juliet had never tied up his tongue before. "Amazing. So beautiful. You're wearing cosmetics."

She blinked sultry eyes and smiled with lips stained the color of deep sunset. Even her height was different. He glanced down. Sexy heels showcased her delicate feet and straps buckled around her ankles highlighted the shapely curve of her legs. He had the sudden mental image of un-buckling those straps with his teeth.

That was it. Dancing was officially a form of torture.

This was all so surreal. She was still the same girl who'd stabbed him in the back but not the same. Tension coiled in his gut, choking off his air supply.

"Thanks. Elise gave me a few tips on how to be a girl." Juliet extended a hand to show off long coral-tipped nails. "Don't expect me to hoist any sails with these babies."

Finn couldn't help but grin. If she was going to play it as if everything was cool, he could too. "I'll do all the hard work. Looking at you is reward enough for my effort."

Her brows rose as she repositioned her hand at his waist. "Like the new me, do you?"

He could feel those nails through his jacket. How was that possible?

"I liked the old you." Before she'd skewered his heart on

the stake of her stubbornness. "But this you is great too. You're gorgeous. What prompted all of this?"

Long nails, swept-up hair. A mouthwatering backless dress he easily recognized as high-end. She was double-take worthy and then some.

"It's part of Elise's deal. She has a lot of high-powered, influential male clients and they expect a certain refinement in their potential mates. She spends a couple of months enhancing each of us, though admittedly, she spent far more time with me than some of the others. *Voila.* I am a new creation. Cinderella, at your service." Juliet glanced at him with a sweeping once-over. "She didn't tell you how all that worked?"

"Not in those terms. It was more of a general guarantee that the woman she matched me with would be able to handle everything that comes with being a princess."

Which, in Juliet's case, had never been a factor. He couldn't have cared less if she flubbed royal protocol or never picked up mascara. Because he'd loved her, once upon a time.

But that was over with a capital *O* and in an arranged marriage, he might as well get what he paid for—a demure, non-scandal-inducing woman who could erase the public's memory of the past year.

"Are you disappointed you got me instead?"

His laugh came out of nowhere. "I honestly don't know what I am, but disappointed is definitely not it."

Juliet could have been a great princess. She'd always understood his need to escape from his position occasionally. Finn gave one hundred percent to his job protecting Delamer's citizens, gladly participated in charity events and didn't have a moment's guilt over taking time away from the public eye. A lot of women wouldn't support that, would insist on being treated to the finer things in life.

Juliet had been perfectly content with a beach date or

sailing. Or staying in, his own personal favorite. No, it wasn't a surprise the computer had matched them.

The surprise lay in how much he still wanted her despite the still-present burn of her betrayal.

"What about you?" he asked. "Has the jury reconvened on whether seeing me again is a pleasant surprise?"

"The jury is busy trying not to trip over your feet while wearing four-inch heels."

The wry twist of her lips pulled an answering grin out of him.

He relaxed. This was still neutral ground and as long as everyone kept a sense of humor, the night was young.

"Let's get some champagne. I'm dying to know how you ended up in Dallas in a matchmaker's computer system."

As they turned to leave the dance floor, light flashed from the crowd to the left and then again in rapid succession. Photographs. From a professional camera.

Finn sighed. With the time difference, his father's phone call would come around midnight unless the king's secretary somehow missed the story, which was unlikely.

Finn would ask Elise to match him with someone new. Later.

Juliet waited until he'd led her to the bar and handed her a flute of bubbly Veuve Clicquot before responding. "It's your fault I sought out Elise."

"Mine?" He dinged the rims of their glasses together and took a healthy swallow in a futile attempt to gain some clarity. "I didn't even know Elise existed until a few days ago."

"It was the engagement announcement. If you were moving on, I needed to, as well. I couldn't do that in Delamer, so here I am." She spread her hands, flashing coral tips that made him imagine what they'd feel like at his waist once he'd shed his jacket and shirt.

The temperature in the ballroom went sky high as internal ripples of need spread. He'd only *thought* he was uncomfortable before.

"Like I said, there's no engagement. Not yet. My father and I agreed it was time I thought about settling down and he went on the bride hunt. Here I am, as well."

It was a sobering reminder. They'd both been trying to move past the scandal and breakup by searching for someone new. Was that what she truly wanted?

The thought of Juliet with another man ripped a hole in his gut. A shock considering how angry he still was about what she'd done.

"As much as I've tried to avoid it, I've seen the pictorial evidence of why your dad thought you needed to settle down. You've become the Party Prince." She shot him a quizzical glance, her gaze flat and unreadable. "It seems so unlike you. Sure, we had some fun dancing at clubs and stuff, but we usually left after an hour or so. Did I miss the part where you wanted to stay?"

"I never wanted to stay. I was always thinking about getting you alone."

"Some of the pictures were really hard to take," she admitted quietly, and he didn't need her to elaborate.

Heat climbed up his neck and flushed across his ears.

He'd always known she'd probably see all the photographs of him with other women and hear about his exploits, but he'd honestly never considered a scenario where they'd have an actual conversation about them. There wasn't a lot about the past year that filled him with pride.

"As long as we're handing out blame, that was *your* fault."

To her credit, she simply glanced at him with a blank expression. "How so?"

She *had* changed. The Juliet of before would have blasted him over such a stupid statement. "Well, not your fault, per se, but I was trying to drown out the memories. Focus on the future. Moving on, like you said."

"Did it work?"

"Not in the slightest."

Their gazes crashed and his lips tingled. He wanted to pull her against him and dive in. Kiss her until neither of them could remember anything other than how good they felt together.

She tossed back the last of her champagne as if she hadn't noticed the heavily charged moment. He wished he could say the same as all the blood rushed from his head, draining southward into a spectacular hard-on.

"What do we do now?" she asked.

"Have dinner with me," he said hoarsely. "Tomorrow night. For old time's sake."

Neither of them thought this match was a good idea. He knew that. But he couldn't resist stealing a few more forbidden hours with Juliet. No matter what she'd done in the past, he couldn't walk out of this ballroom and never see her again.

"I should have my head examined. But okay."

Her acceptance was fortuitously timed. A svelte woman and her friend nearly bowled Juliet over in an enthusiastic attempt to get a photo with him.

It was a common-enough request and he normally didn't mind. But tonight he wanted to be selfish and spend as much time with Juliet as he could, before his father interfered. Before all the reasons they'd split in the first place surfaced.

She'd always be the woman who burned a Delamer flag at the palace gates. The people of his country had long memories for acts of disloyalty to the crown.

And so did he.

There was no way crossing an ocean could create a different dynamic between two people. Because Juliet would never see he couldn't go against his father, and never understand that as the second son, Finn had little to offer the crown besides unconditional support.

If she ever did finally get it, all her sins would be forgiven. By everyone, including him.

That would happen when it snowed in Delamer dur-ing July.

Until then, he'd indulge in Juliet, ignore the rest and then ask Elise to match him with someone else.

Three

Juliet stared in the mirror and tried to concentrate on applying eye shadow to her lids as Dannie and Elise had shown her. Multiple times. Her scrambled brain couldn't focus.

Dazed and breathless well described the state Finn had left her in last night, and it hadn't cleared up in the almost twenty-four hours since. Finn's clean scent lingered in her nose, evoking painfully crisp memories of being with him, loving him.

And suffering the agony of finally accepting that he cared nothing for her. Cared nothing for her pain at losing the brother she'd helped raise.

All Finn cared about was zipping himself into the uniform of Delamer's military and wearing it with nationalistic pride.

Madness. Why had she agreed to this date again?

Elise stuck her head in the door of Juliet's room.

"Almost ready? Oh. You're not even dressed yet. What are you wearing?"

A flak jacket if she was smart. And if they made one you could wear internally. But she'd come to America in hopes of finding a new direction. She'd stay open to the possibility that time had dulled Finn's zealous fervor.

One date. One night. What did she have to lose?

Her eyes narrowed. She'd stay open, but that didn't mean Finn didn't deserve to suffer for his sins.

"I want to wear something that will show Finn what I've endured in your makeover program because of him. The sexier and more painful for him, the better." Hours and hours of hot rollers, facials and balancing on four-inch heels were about to hit his royal highness where it hurt.

"Yellow dress, then. I brought you something." Elise held out a velvet jewelry box.

Mystified, Juliet opened the lid to reveal a silver heart charm dangling from a matching chain, and another heart dangled from the first, one clutching the other to keep it from falling. "It's beautiful. Thank you."

Simple but elegant, perfect for a tomboy who'd rather be doing something athletic than primping.

Elise clasped it around Juliet's throat. "I give all my makeover clients a necklace. I'm glad you like it."

When the hired car with dark windows rolled to a stop outside Elise's house, Juliet was slightly ashamed to realize she'd been haunting the window for nearly fifteen minutes waiting for its appearance. How pathetic.

She swung open Elise's front door, and the sheer heat in the pointed once-over Finn gave her swept everything else away.

"Hi."

"Wow," was all he said in response.

Little pinpricks worked their way across her cheeks in a stupid blush. "Yeah? It's okay? Elise picked out the dress."

And what was under it, but odds were slim this date would go well enough to model the silk lingerie.

In answer, he grasped her hand and led her out of the house. "I like what I see so far. Come with me so I can properly evaluate the rest."

Her arm tingled from his touch against her palm, warming her in places Finn had always affected quite expertly.

Whom was she kidding? Finn was nothing if not talented enough to get her out of the sunny yellow dress and ivory alligator sandals in less than five minutes if he so chose.

She let him hold her hand down the walk. Partially because she wanted to pretend things were somewhat normal. That this was a date with an exciting man who was whirling her off to a night of possibilities.

He tucked her into the backseat of the luxurious town car and settled in next to her, his heavy masculine presence overwhelming in such close confines. She almost jumped out of her skin when he leaned forward, brushing her arm and setting off a throng of iron-winged butterflies in her stomach. But he only pressed the button to raise the dividing panel between the driver and the back, lingering far too long for such a simple task.

The car slid smoothly away from the curb and flowed into traffic.

"Where are you taking me?" she croaked and cleared the awareness and heat from her throat. "Some place trendy and hip?"

"Not on your life. I'm not sharing you with hordes of paparazzi and gawkers."

Oh. "Are your bodyguards in another car? They're never far away unless you're working."

He squeezed the hand he was still holding. "Worried? I'll keep you safe."

Without a doubt. It was what he did. Most people ignored those in distress, but he reveled in protecting people. Always had.

They chatted about inane topics such as Dallas weather, but thankfully, he did not mention football. The only sport he'd ever followed was Formula 1 racing, but he respected her complete boredom with cars looping a track and seldom talked about it.

"We're here," Finn pronounced as the car stopped under a tree.

Juliet took in the scene through the window. Beyond the roadway lay a secluded private park, where a single table and chairs had been set out with a perfect view of the sunset. A man in a tall white chef's hat stood off to the side, chopping with a flashing knife on a temporary work surface.

"Nice," Juliet acknowledged with a nod and peeked up at Finn from under her lashes. "Out of curiosity, what would you have done if it was raining?"

"We'd get wet. Or we'd ride around and look for a drive-through with decent takeout and eat in the car."

She smiled at his pragmatism. He'd never let a little thing like a change of plans put a hitch in his stride. "Then I'm glad it's a clear night."

His answering grin warmed her neglected parts far past acceptability.

"After the obscene amount of money I paid to rent this park for the night, including an added fifteen percent to buy out the existing reservation, it wouldn't dare rain."

No, it wouldn't. Rain didn't fall on the head of the privileged. Once, he'd made her feel as if the evils of the world couldn't reach them, as if he'd always be the one person she could count on. Until he wasn't.

Finn jumped from the car and helped her rise from the low leather seat. The driver sped away after being told to return in two hours. They were alone.

Juliet started to walk up the path to the center of the park.

Finn tugged on her hand, swinging her around face-to-face. "Maybe we should get something out of the way."

"What's that?" The words were half out of her mouth when the sizzle between them and the glint of anticipation in his blue eyes answered that question.

He was going to kiss her.

Involuntarily, her tongue came out to wet suddenly dry lips and his eyes lingered on them before he met her gaze squarely.

"This."

Juliet froze as Finn's mouth descended.

A part of her screamed to break his hold, to run before it was too late. Her legs wouldn't move.

Then his lips claimed hers, taking her mouth powerfully, demanding a response. It was *Finn*. So familiar and hot and everything she'd been missing for a very long time. She moaned and leaned into it, desperate to taste the divine, to plunge into him.

Euphoria rushed through her veins, deluging her senses with sharp, slick desire. Pushing eager fingers through his short hair, she held his head in place as the kiss exploded with incandescent energy.

Their bodies melded, aligning just right, just as always. *Yes.* Oh, yes, she'd missed him.

Missed how he never held back, missed his intoxicating presence and missed how his strength enabled hers.

His hand slipped beneath a spaghetti strap at her shoulder and he skimmed silky fingertips down her back. If he kept this up, her lingerie would be making an appearance after all, very shortly.

He pulled away before she'd even begun to sate herself on the thrill of his touch. Breathing heavily, he rested his forehead on hers. "That didn't quite do what I hoped."

It had certainly done plenty for her. "What were you hoping for?"

"That it would allow me to eat in peace instead of thinking about whether you still taste the same. Now I'm pretty sure a repeat is all I'll be thinking about."

She hid a smile. "If dinner goes well, a repeat might be on the menu."

His eyelids dropped to a sexy, slumberous half-mast. "I'll keep that in mind. Shall we eat?"

"If you insist." He might be able to eat. The flip-flopping in her stomach didn't bode well for her.

There were still plenty of sparks between them. Not that she'd wondered. But that kiss had at least answered one lingering question—whether they could pick up where they'd left off.

The answer was a resounding yes.

As long as they could sort through the past. The scandal. The utter sense of betrayal he'd left her with.

Suddenly, she didn't want to think about it. There weren't any laws that said they had to immediately hash out how abandoned she'd felt.

Finn led her to a chair and helped her sit, then took his own seat. As the chef served a delicious first course of tomatoes drizzled with balsamic vinegar, Finn mentioned the queen's bout with appendicitis and Juliet murmured appropriate well-wishes. She then shared that her second-youngest sister was expecting a baby and nodded at Finn's hearty congratulations.

A very pleasant conversation all the way around. Thankfully, at least some of the social graces Elise had tirelessly drilled into Juliet's head had held.

Except she couldn't get that kiss out of her mind, and watching him talk wasn't helping. It had been a very long time since she'd been kissed. Since the scandal.

Finn hadn't let any grass grow under his feet in the female companionship department, but she'd taken the ostrich approach. If she stuck her head in the sand long enough, all those feminine urges would dry up and go away.

She'd been pretty successful thus far. Yet in two seconds, he'd done a spectacular job of reminding her sheer will couldn't stop the flood of longing for the tender affections of one very talented prince.

"Did you quit your job in Delamer?" Finn asked once the chef finished serving the main course of corvina sea bass and asparagus over quinoa.

"I did."

The short phrase communicated none of the grief she'd experienced over resigning her position teaching English to bright young minds. She loved the children she taught and had hoped to find a way to continue teaching in America.

Then she remembered.

She hadn't been matched with an American husband. If things worked out with Finn, she could go home, go back to her job, back to the sea. Back into his arms.

Was such a fairy tale actually possible?

With renewed interest, she swept her gaze over the man opposite her. "Are you still flying helicopters?"

"Of course. I'll do that until the day I die. Or until they ground me. Whichever comes first."

No shock. He'd always loved flying as much as he did the search and rescue part of his job. The source of contention wasn't *what* he did but whom he did it for.

"Hmm," she said noncommittally and forked up a bite of fish. "I wasn't going to jump right into this, but I'm on uncertain ground here. Tell me what you hoped to gain from Elise's match. Are you really looking for a wife?"

Finn set his wineglass down firmly and focused on her, the warmth in his expression all too easy to read. "I can't keep being the Party Prince. The best I thought I could do was an arranged marriage, like my parents. Means to an end, and I'm okay with that. What about you?"

That focus unleashed a shiver she couldn't quite control. "I was prepared to marry whomever Elise picked. I couldn't stay in Delamer. Not with the way things fell apart between us. Marriage was a means to an end for me, as well."

She'd like to stop there and just enjoy this date. But there were too many unanswered questions for that.

"What is this dinner all about? We aren't having a first date like we would with the matches we'd envisioned for ourselves. This is something else. We have history we're avoiding. Important history. History that has to be resolved."

Finn's gaze grew keen. "You want to throw down? Go for it."

"No, I don't." She shook her head, though he was certainly the only man who could take whatever she dished out. "We've fought enough in our relationship. I want to work things out like adults. Can we?"

With a smile, Finn picked up her hand and rubbed a knuckle with his smooth thumb. "Let's hold off on history with a capital *H*. Dinner is about me and you reconnecting. That's the part of our history I prefer to remember."

"Okay."

She'd waited this long. What were a few more hours? The time would be well spent working through what she'd realized she'd done wrong a year ago. Instead of fighting so hard to convince Finn to talk to his father, she should have gone about this a whole different way.

If Finn was truly looking for a wife, what was stopping her from marrying him in order to bring about change from inside the palace gates? Princess Juliet would have far more power to influence the king away from mandatory military service than plain old Juliet Villere.

And then maybe she could finally be rid of the crushing guilt she felt over Bernard's death.

Dinner forgotten, Finn nearly swallowed his tongue when Juliet pushed back her chair and waltzed to his side of the table wearing a sultry smile and sporting a very naughty glint in her eye. She extended a hand, which he took silently, and then he stood, allowing her to lead him up the path into a more heavily wooded section of the park.

"Interested in the native fauna and flora?" he asked when the silence stretched on.

"More interested in how well the flora conceals us." She backed him up against a tree and stepped into his torso deliberately, rubbing her firm breasts against his chest.

Oh, so *that's* what she had in mind. Obviously, she remembered how good it had been as well as he did. And apparently she had no problem rekindling that part of their relationship, impending matches to other people notwithstanding. Fantastic.

"That earlier kiss was good. Make this one better," she commanded.

Instantly, he complied, yanking her into his arms and exploring her back flat-handed. Their mouths met, aligning perfectly, and heat arced between them.

Juliet.

Desire thundered through his body, soaking him with a storm of need. She was in his arms, overpowering his senses as if he'd jumped from his helicopter without a parachute.

Thank God Elise had pulled her devious stunt to put them in each other's path again, if only for one night. Tomorrow, he and Juliet could both be matched with more suitable mates.

The kiss deepened and Juliet snuggled against him as if she'd never been away. Heat swept along his skin, craving the perfection of Juliet's beautiful body against it. He groaned and shifted a knee between her legs, and his thigh hit the sweet spot immediately.

That was some dress. The high-heeled and insanely sexy shoes helped too.

He lifted his lips a fraction and murmured, "I've missed you. Can we take this someplace more private?"

Her smile curved against his cheek and she nodded.

Grasping her hand, he pulled her in the direction of the newly returned town car, settled her in the backseat and nearly dived in after her.

He'd never been able to resist her, and now he didn't have to.

Somehow, Finn had been granted a reprieve. The king hadn't phoned him to demand an explanation for the photographs from last night. Now he had this one chance to recapture a small slice of heaven before submitting to an arranged marriage.

He'd hoped, against all logical reason, that the woman Elise matched him with could heal his broken heart. The odds of that happening with the woman who'd smashed it in the first place were zilch. Especially since he'd never in a million years give it to her again.

So he'd grant EA International another chance. Once he had a new bride by his side, the public would forget about the Party Prince and he could become known for something worthwhile.

The People's Prince. He liked the sound of that.

In the meantime, he could have Juliet…and all the good things about their relationship. Without getting into the painful past.

"So I take it you thought dinner went well?" he asked with a grin he couldn't have wiped off his face for anything. "You know, since you agreed to a repeat of the kiss."

Her hair was a little mussed from his fingers. He itched to pull out all the pins and let those silky locks tumble over him.

"I'm staying open to where the night leads. But it's been good so far." She studied him speculatively. "We're not fighting. We're connecting, like you said."

They weren't fighting because they'd thus far avoided the problem. And he was totally prepared to keep avoiding history with a capital *H* for as long as possible. "If this driver would step on it, we'd be connecting a whole lot more."

She laughed. "We have all night. But while we're on the subject, does connecting mean you're open to being on my side this time around?"

Apparently she did not subscribe to the same desire for avoidance of the past. "I've always been on your side."

"If that was true, you'd never have taken the stance you did." Her expression closed in. "You'd have supported me and my family when we tried to talk to your father."

That was the Juliet he'd last seen in Delamer. His stomach dipped. The connection part of the evening appeared to be over.

"You say that like I had no choice, like I had to agree with you or it equaled lack of support." But that's how he'd felt, as well. As if she couldn't see his side. Instantly, it all came roaring back. All the hurt and anger he'd been living with for a very long year. "You didn't support me either. And I never asked you to go against everything you believed in."

She yanked her hand from his. The heat in her expression reminded him she got just as passionate about taking his head off when they clashed.

So much for dinner going well.

"That's exactly what you wanted me to do." A lone tear tracked down Juliet's face and his gut clenched. It hurt to see someone as strong as Juliet crying. "Forget about Bernard and support you every day as you put on the uniform of the Delamer military. Every day, I'd be reminded Bernard died wearing the same uniform and I did nothing to avenge that. Every day, I'd be reminded you chose to stand with the crown instead of with me."

The car stopped at the private entrance to his hotel. It was positioned discreetly in the secluded rear section of the property, off to the side of the underground parking garage.

Finn didn't get out. This wasn't finished, not even close.

"Vengeance well describes it. You humiliated me. That protest garnered the attention of the entire world. Juliet—" Finn pinched the bridge of his nose. They should have recorded this conversation and played it back, saving them the trouble of having it again. "I'm a member of the House of Couronne. You burned the flag of the country my family rules *while we were dating.* How can you not see what that did to me?"

Not to mention the man she'd vilified was his *father.* He loved his father, loved his country. She'd wanted him to choose her over honor.

"My family is forever changed because of your father's policies. Bernard is gone and—" Her voice seized, choking off the rest. After a moment, she stared up at him through watery eyes laced with devastation. "A man who claimed to love me would have understood. He would have done anything to make that right."

But he wasn't just a man and never would be. He could no sooner remove the royal blood in his veins than he could fly blindfolded.

The tearing in his chest felt as if it was on repeat, as well. "A woman who claimed to love me would have realized I have an obligation to the crown, whether it's on my head or not. I don't get the choice to be someone other than Prince Alain Phineas of Montagne, Duke of Marechal, House of Couronne."

He belonged to one of the last royal houses of Europe and he owed it to his ancestors to preserve the country they'd left in his care. No matter how antiquated the notion became in an increasingly modern world.

Now he was ready to get out of the car. To be somewhere she wasn't. That was one thing that hadn't changed—Juliet causing him to feel a touch insane as he veered between extreme highs and lows very quickly. She followed him to the curb, clearly determined to continue twisting the spike through his heart.

"I never wanted you to be someone else. I loved *you*."

Past tense. It didn't escape his notice.

"You meant everything to me, Finn. But it's peacetime. The mandatory military service law is ridiculous. Why can't you see that your royal obligation is to stop being so stubborn and think about people's lives?"

"For the same reason you can't see that the military is mine," he said quietly.

He'd never wear the crown. Flying helicopters was the one thing he could do that Alexander, as the crown prince, couldn't. Juliet's refusal to get out from under her righteous indignation prevented *her* from taking *his* side.

She was the stubborn one.

Anger coated the back of his throat. Juliet was still the same crusader under the cosmetics and sexy dress. She was still determined to alter the heart of the institution to which he'd sworn loyalty.

Suddenly, it was all too easy to resist her. He didn't have the slightest interest in rehashing all of this for the rest of the night, regardless of the more tangible rewards. He'd never bowed to anyone before and he wasn't about to start now.

Arms crossed against her abdomen, Juliet stared dry-eyed at the unoccupied valet booth behind Finn. "I think it's safe to say the date was not a success."

"I'll have the driver take you back to Elise's house." Finn tapped on the passenger-side window.

The squeal of tires on cement reverberated through the quiet underground lot. A van sped down the ramp and wedged tight against the rear bumper of Finn's hired car. Four men with distinctly shaved heads, beefy physiques and dark clothing jumped out, trouble written all over them.

"Juliet, get in the car," Finn muttered, angling his body to shield her as the men advanced on them.

He never should have given his security guys the night off.

It was the last thing he registered as the world went black.

Four

Grit scraped at Juliet's eyeballs. She tried to lift a hand to rub them. And couldn't.

Heavy fog weighed down her brain. Something was wrong. She couldn't see and her hands weren't working. Or her arms.

Rapid blinking didn't improve her eyesight. It was so *dark*.

She never drank enough alcohol to be this fuzzy about her current whereabouts…and how she'd gotten there… and what had happened prior to.

"Juliet. Can you hear me?" Finn's voice. It washed over her, tripping a hodgepodge of memories, most of them X-rated.

Finn's voice in the dark equaled one activity and one activity only. Pleasure, the feel of his skin on hers, urgency of the highest order to fly into the heavens with him—

Wait. What was *Finn* doing here?

"Yeah," she mumbled thickly. "I hear you."

Pain split through her brain the moment her jaw moved, cutting off her speech, her thoughts, even her breath. Inhaling sharply, she rolled to shift positions—or tried to.

Her muscles refused to cooperate. "What's…going on?"

"Tranquilizer," Finn explained grimly and spit out a nasty curse in French. "I think they must have used the same dose on both of us."

The sinister-looking men. An unmarked van. The date with so much promise that ended badly. And then got worse.

Juliet groaned. "What? Why did they give us tranquilizers?"

"So they could snatch us without a fight," Finn growled. "And they should be thanking their lucky stars they did. Otherwise I would have removed their spleens with a tire iron."

Snippets of dinner with Finn flashed through her mind. Okay, good. So she hadn't lost her memory and she wasn't suffering from the effects of a hangover. "We were kidnapped? Stuff like that only happens in the movies."

"Welcome to reality." The heavy sarcasm meant he was frustrated. And maybe a little worried. That didn't bode well. Finn always knew what to do.

Shifting along her right side indicated his general vicinity. Not too far away. "Can you move? Are we tied up?"

It was hard for her to tell. Everything was numb. That's why she couldn't move. She'd been *drugged*. And blinded, maybe forever.

What sort of scheme had she stumbled into simply by being in the wrong place at the wrong time with the wrong companion?

A strong, masculine hand smoothed hair from her face, throwing her back to another time and place where that happened with frequency.

"Nah," Finn said. "They shot us up with enough narcotics that they didn't need to tie us up. I'm okay. The cocktail didn't affect me nearly as long as it did you."

Gray invaded her vision and got lighter and lighter with each passing moment. Thank goodness. "Where are we?"

"Not sure. In a house of some sort. I was afraid to leave you alone in case you needed CPR, or the welcoming committee showed up, so I didn't do more than look out the window."

A fuzzy Finn swam through her eyesight, along with a few background details. White walls. Bed.

Finn held her hand. She squeezed, gratified that her fingers had actually responded, and then licked dry lips. "Guards?"

"Not that I can tell. I haven't seen anyone since I regained consciousness." Finn nodded to a door. "As soon as you can walk, we'll see what's what."

"Help me sit up," she implored him.

Finn's arm came around her waist and she slumped against him. Two tries later, her legs swung off the bed and thumped to the floor.

Barefoot. Had they taken her shoes? She wasn't even completely over the sticker shock at the price of those ivory alligator sandals and now they were probably in a Dumpster somewhere. And she'd actually kind of liked them.

"Now help me stand," she said. Their captors might return at any moment and they both needed to be prepared. Sure Finn was stronger and better trained, but she was mad enough to take out at least one.

Finn shook his head. "There's no prize for Fastest Recovery After Being Tranquilized. Take your time."

"I want to get out of here. The faster we figure out what that's going to take, the better." Throbbing behind her eyes distracted her for a moment, but she ignored it as best she could. "How far do you think they took us from your hotel?"

Elise would be worried. Maybe she'd already called the

police and even now, SWAT teams were tearing apart Dallas in search of Prince Alain.

Or…Elise might be smugly certain she'd staged the match of the century and assume they'd gotten so wrapped up in each other, Juliet had forgotten to call. The matchmaker probably didn't realize they were missing yet.

"There's only one way to find out where we are. Come on." Finn took one step and her knees buckled.

Without missing a beat, he swept her up in his strong arms and she almost sighed at the shamefully romantic gesture.

Except he was still the Prince of Pigheadedness. Why had she ever thought she could marry him—even under the guise of changing Delamer policy from the inside?

Finn deposited her easily on the pale blue counterpane and kept a light but firm hand on her shoulder so she couldn't sit up. "It's early afternoon, if the daylight outside the window is any indication. We've probably been captives for about eighteen hours. The entire Delamer armed forces are likely already on their way to assist the local authorities. Stay here and I'll go figure out the lay of the land."

"You're not the boss just because you're a boy."

He scowled. "I'm not trying to be the boss. I'm trying to keep you from cracking your stubborn head open. If you think you can walk, be my guest."

With a flourish, he gestured toward the door.

Now she had to do it, if for no other reason than to prove His Highness wrong. Slowly, she wobbled upright and took excruciatingly slow steps, one in front of the other.

The door opened easily, despite her certainty that she'd find it locked. It swung open to reveal a bare hallway. "Let's go."

She'd almost taken an entire step across the threshold when Finn leaped in front like her own personal bulletproof vest.

She rolled her eyes. Of course. Bullets bounced off the perpetually arrogant all the time, right?

"Don't you have any sense?" he growled in her ear. "This is a dangerous situation."

If the kidnappers had wanted to harm them, they would have. Finn was more valuable alive than dead. "If anything dangerous is lurking in these halls, it's going to get you first. Then who will protect me?"

"What makes you so certain I'd lose?" he whispered over his shoulder as he flowed noiselessly away from the bedroom. He'd always moved with elegant flair, but this cloak-and-dagger-style grace was sexier than she'd like to admit.

She dogged his steps, tearing her gaze from his spectacular backside with difficulty. "A hunch. If the kidnappers had tranquilizers, they probably have guns. Unless you think they're in this for the opportunity to have afternoon tea with royalty."

"Shh." He halted where the hallway ended in a large room and poked his head out to scan the space with a double sweep. "All clear."

An inviting living area with a fireplace and high-end furniture opened up around her as she stepped out of the hall. "This is not what I would have envisioned as a place to keep captives."

A breathtaking panorama of sparkling sea unfolded beyond a wall of glass. The house perched on a low cliff overlooking the water. That particular shade of blue was etched on her heart, and her breath caught.

"We're not in Dallas anymore," Finn announced needlessly. "And those were some serious drugs the kidnappers used if they brought us clear across the Atlantic without me realizing it."

"We're on an island."

She was home. Back on the Mediterranean, close to everything she loved. She'd sailed these waters often enough to recognize the hills rising behind the city, the coastal landscape.

Home. She never thought she'd see it again. The small ripples in the surface of the water. The wheeling birds. The sky studded with puffy clouds. All of the poetic nuances of the sea bled into her chest, squeezing it, nearly wrenching loose a sob.

"Yeah." Finn skirted the large couch and squinted at the shoreline visible in the distance. "About two miles off the coast of Delamer. There are, I don't know, at least four or five different islands in this quadrant. It's hard to tell from the ground which one we're on."

"There can't be more than a handful of people who own houses on these islands. It would be pretty easy to figure out who kidnapped us." She shook her head. "We were taken by the dumbest kidnappers ever. They dumped us right in our own backyard."

"Dumb—or really smart. Who would think to look for us here? We're both supposed to be in Dallas."

"Well…good point."

So if all the search efforts were concentrated on the other side of the Atlantic, they were going to have to rescue themselves.

"And leaving us on an island means they don't have to stick around," she said. "Very difficult for us to escape. I assume they took both our cell phones."

He nodded. "And I'm sure the kidnappers did a full sweep to remove all devices with access to the outside world."

Gingerly, he gripped the handle of the sliding door and pulled. It slid open, and the swift Mediterranean breeze doused her with its unique marine-life-drenched tang.

Goodness how she'd missed it.

She followed Finn outside onto the covered flagstone patio, set with wicker outdoor furniture around a brick fire pit. The cry of gulls overhead was like hearing a favorite

song for the first time in ages. There were worse places
to be held captive than in a cliff-side villa in the south of
France during early summer.

But they were still captives.

Finn gripped the wrought iron railing surrounding the
patio and peered down the cliff to the rocky shore below.
"The slip is empty."

Sure enough, the dock was boat-free. "Maybe there's
a kayak or something in storage that the kidnappers forgot about."

"We should definitely check around. I'm still not convinced we're alone." Finn grimaced. "Why would they
leave us unsupervised in what's essentially a vacation spot?
None of this makes any sense."

"Kidnapping as a whole doesn't make any sense. How
is kidnapping you, and by extension me, going to achieve
changes in the king's policies?"

Even in the midst of her lowest point of grief over Bernard's death, she'd have never willingly put another human
in harm's way to promote her political agenda.

"One would assume we're being held for ransom." Finn
shot her a wry sideways glance. "Not everyone is a crusader, you know. Though I find it a bit endearing you immediately jumped to the conclusion that the motive here
is political gain."

Her spine stiffened. Why didn't he call her naive too,
while he was at it? "You don't have to make fun of me. I
get that you don't agree with me."

"I'm not making fun of you. I was being dead serious. Your passion for your principles is one of my favorite
things about you."

He tipped her chin up to force her gaze to his.

She let him and blamed it on her half-tranquilized brain.
But no quantity of numbing agents could stop the flutter
in her chest when he looked at her with his eyes all liquid

and bottomless and beautiful. Worse, it was clear he was telling the truth.

She looked away without comment. Because really, what could she say to that? It was the perfect encapsulation of their relationship. He appreciated her passion but not what she was passionate about. She loved his sense of loyalty but not what he swore allegiance to.

His hand fell to his side and he stared out over the water as if engrossed by the view.

The endless vicious circle they'd been plunged into could never be broken, and the crushing sadness of it gripped her insides anew.

Maybe she should catch a clue from the kidnappers. They'd exhibited a ruthless determination to reach their goals—whatever those goals might be—and she could do the same.

Not everyone was a crusader, but it took only one to upset the status quo.

For Bernard.

If she eliminated her emotions from the equation, perhaps she could still figure out a way to get the reform she wanted. First, she had to figure out how to get off this island.

Finn laced his fingers at the back of his neck to keep from reaching for Juliet again. She obviously didn't welcome his touch. He understood why—the storm of last night's argument still lingered between them.

But he'd been forced to watch her ashen face for an eternity, praying she'd wake up soon. Praying their captors didn't return with unsavory appetites. He didn't have a problem doing others bodily harm to protect Juliet, but he liked it better when he didn't have to.

Now that she was awake, he had a nearly incontrollable urge to fold her into his embrace and assure himself she was really okay.

She cleared her throat. "We should split up and search the property for a boat."

Obviously she was on the road to recovery.

"Are you out of your mind? Why on earth would you think I'd let you out of my sight?"

She'd just made an excellent point about men with guns, and she thought splitting up was a good plan?

Scowling, she tied her hair up in messy knot, as if preparing to wade into a brawl. "Because we need to get off this island in a hurry and we'll search faster if we do it separately."

"We're not splitting up," he growled. "Walk fast and that'll achieve the same end."

With a withering glare, she took off down the stairs bolted to the cliff side, and her pace was a clear dare-you-to-keep-up. He scrambled after her, easily matching her long-legged stride until they hit sea level. Wordlessly, they tramped over the rocky shoreline and he clamped his mouth closed lest he accidentally show some concern for the sharp rocks digging into her bare feet.

If she'd slow down a minute, he might have volunteered the location of her shoes—in the closet of the room where she'd slept off the tranquilizer. Though the sexy spiked heels probably weren't the best choice for beach-tramping.

"There's nothing here," she said, hands on her hips. The breeze pulled stands of hair from the knot at her nape, wrapping them around her face and neck.

His blood pumped faster as he took in the sight.

Did she have any idea how beautiful she was? Especially framed by the homeland and sea he loved.

He still wanted to sweep her into his arms and forget everything else but pleasure.

He glanced away. "There's a lot of island left to cover. Don't give up yet."

"I wasn't giving up. I was reevaluating. We should be looking for some way to start a fire. Surely there are people out on the water, and someone is doing your job in your place, right? Smoke signals are a better bet than searching for a boat."

"That's a good idea," he lied.

It would never work. Everyone knew the dozens of small islands off the coast of Delamer were owned by wealthy, influential people. Who would dare intrude on someone's private domain to investigate what they'd assume was a bonfire on the beach?

But it was better than doing nothing.

They climbed the stairs to the patio. In the lavishly appointed kitchen, Finn slung open cabinets and drawers in search of matches or a lighter.

Juliet poked her head out of the walk-in pantry. "Well, if we aren't rescued soon, at least we won't starve. Come see this. There are enough provisions in here to feed all your coast guard buddies for a month."

It was the second time she'd mentioned his job in less than ten minutes, and derision laced her tone without apology. She didn't see anything wrong with disparaging a profession he loved.

He wanted to wring her neck as much as he wanted her naked. Push-pull. Seemed as if he'd never escape it.

He swallowed the frustration and joined her. True to her description, boxes and jars lined the shelves of the well-stocked pantry. Cereal, pasta, canned beans and fruits—nearly every variety of dry goods he could imagine.

Curious now, he exited to the kitchen and pulled open the double doors of the stainless steel refrigerator. "Same here. Our captors went to great lengths to ensure we'd have three square meals a day."

The refrigerator held steaks, chicken breasts, fresh vegetables and staples such as milk and butter, all unopened and unexpired.

Juliet brushed his arm as she came up beside him to

peer into the interior. "It makes me uneasy. How long are they expecting to keep us here?"

Worry lined her face, which was still a little white. Most of her makeup had worn off, allowing her true beauty to shine through. He hated seeing it marred by stress.

"Wish I knew." Frustration returned in a rush. With it came the "if-onlys": *If only I hadn't given Gomez and La-Salle the night off. If only I'd invited Juliet to dinner in my hotel room. If only I'd had five more seconds to react when the van pulled up.*

That was a sure way to get his temper in a knot and resolve exactly nothing.

"Why don't you check over near the fireplace for matches?"

The farther away she was, the less she could affect his senses.

As she left the kitchen, he shoved both hands in his pockets. Paper crinkled under his knuckles and he withdrew an envelope with the king's seal prominently displayed in the center. An envelope that hadn't been in his pocket last night.

A strange sense of foreboding slid along Finn's spine.

He slipped an index finger under the seal and withdrew the folded page, his mind already piecing together aspects of this odd kidnapping plot into a whole he didn't like.

Exactly as he suspected, the page bore a note written in his father's bold hand.

Sorry to inconvenience you, blah, blah, but unexpected events caused me to reevaluate blah, blah.

Finn's gaze zeroed in on the last paragraph:

The Villere family is gaining traction in turning public opinion against my rule. Use this time I'm giving you with Juliet well. Patch things up with her and use your relationship to influence both her and her family into dropping their inflammatory political campaign. Marry her and en-

*sure it's clear the Villere family sides with the crown. It's
the most advantageous match for everyone.*

Now Finn knew why he'd never heard from his father
about the photographs from Elise's party.

The king had orchestrated a kidnapping plot instead.

Finn's throat tightened. No wonder their captors had
left them unsupervised in paradise. It was forced seclusion
so Finn had the opportunity to seduce Juliet into siding
with him instead of her family. Kidnapping allowed Finn
to claim innocence in the deal, and furthermore allowed
them to commiserate as they endured their circumstances.

It was fiendishly ingenious. And insane.

The paper crumbled in Finn's fist. His father had gone
too far. Juliet had been drugged, not to mention frightened.
For what? So Finn could perform a miracle and make Juliet
an advocate of the crown? If that was possible, he'd have
done it a year ago.

"Found the matches," she called with the most cheer
she'd exhibited since coming out of unconsciousness.

Matches were totally unnecessary given this new de-
velopment. No one was looking for them.

No one would take the slightest bit of notice of a plume
of smoke coming from this island, which he now knew
for certain was Île de Etienne, where Alexander and Portia owned the only house occupying the entire hunk of
rock. This luxurious cage doubled as a lover's retreat for
the crown prince and his wife, which was why Finn had
never been invited to check it out.

Was his brother in on the plot too? Was everyone in
the royal family waiting to see how Finn would handle
this twist?

The best way to combat the king's underhanded tactics
was to tell Juliet exactly what was going on.

"A fire isn't going to help. Listen, you need to—"

"No, you listen." She scowled. "You don't know everything because you're in the military. You can sit around

here and wait for your buddies to show up, but I'm not going to. I want to go home."

Turning on her heel, she flounced from the kitchen, her gorgeous backside swinging under her crinkled but still very sexy yellow dress. The shush of the sliding door opening and then being shut—likely with Juliet on the outside—reverberated in the suddenly quiet house.

Finn sank onto a bar stool with a groan and put his aching head in his palms. What an obstinate, hardheaded woman. Those very qualities had caused him immeasurable pain a year ago, and only an idiot would step up for a repeat.

The last thing he wanted to do was chase after her, and the only silver lining in this situation was that he didn't have to. If nothing else, the king's note reassured Finn they weren't in any danger from zealous criminals who might return at any moment to start slicing off fingers.

What had the king been thinking? Well, that wasn't a mystery. It was all there in blue fountain pen. Finn had an opportunity to make an advantageous match, exactly as his father had discussed before sending Finn off to Dallas. It was merely the definition of "advantageous" that had changed.

If it hadn't been happening to him, Finn might have appreciated the brilliance of the move. With no access to the outside world, Juliet wouldn't realize her family was turning the tide in their quest to see someone pay for Bernard's death. Furthermore, the king surely knew he was playing to Finn's sense of honor and duty to the crown.

Hands flat on the bar, Finn shoved to his feet. He would not be an active party to deceiving Juliet, especially not to the point of marrying her and then influencing her to side against her family. *Influence* was code for *coerce*. Their differences could only be truly resolved if she chose him willingly.

And that wasn't happening. She was far too stubborn and she still made him far too angry.

Finn went outside, determined to tell Juliet what the king had done. Then, they could work together to escape this ridiculous plot.

Smoke plumed from the rocky shore. He peered over the cliff's edge. Juliet stood near a blazing wood patio chair, turned upside down on the ground. Apparently his brother would be short a piece or two of furniture the next time he was in residence, which was Alexander's due for lending the house to their father's scheme.

"Any luck?" Finn called as he descended the stairs.

"Yeah, can't you see the Delamer armed forces storming the beach?" she retorted, throwing his earlier words back at him. "You must not be as important as you think since no one's come to rescue us yet."

Actually, he was *more* important than he'd thought, which was why they were both in this situation. "I tried to tell you a fire wouldn't work."

"Feel free to come up with a plan that will work, Genius."

He opened his mouth to blurt out the truth. Something in her posture, or the wind, or something beating through his chest stopped him.

He was important.

More important than he'd realized.

The king wasn't pushing chess pieces across his royal board—this situation had been carefully constructed to allow Finn to shape the future of Delamer. His brother couldn't do this. Neither could his father. Only Finn had a prayer of swaying Juliet and her family away from their attacks on the king and the Delamer military.

Finn, the second son, wasn't useless after all.

The king possessed a sharper mind than Finn had credited. If Finn told Juliet about the king's involvement in the kidnapping, it would only fuel her ire. Who knew what she'd do to retaliate? The goal was to get her to stop disparaging his family, not make it worse.

Furthermore, if Finn *didn't* do as his father asked, the king might find another way to handle the problem of Juliet and her family, a way that could potentially destroy their lives.

Finn alone held all the winning cards.

If he did as his father asked, he'd save his country and have Juliet again. In his life, in his bed. But never in his heart. That part of their relationship was over.

Juliet stared out over the water, her face troubled.

"I'm racking my brain for a plan," he told her. Which was true enough…but it wasn't a rescue plan. It looked a lot more like a seduction plan. But could he really go through with it?

Glancing at Juliet, he fingered the crushed note out of his pocket and dropped it into the fire. The paper curled, turned black and then burst into flames.

If only his misgivings about the task before him were so easily destroyed.

Five

Finn coughed away a bit of smoke. "So, here's a plan. Let's go back to the house and eat. We'll talk about next steps once we've fueled up."

The reprieve would also give him time to think through what he wanted to do. Could he really seduce Juliet out of her position against the king's military policies?

He'd been convinced at dinner last night she hadn't changed, but in their year apart, she'd quit a job she loved, flew across the Atlantic and enrolled in a matchmaker program with the intent to marry an American.

Obviously *some* things had changed. But enough things? Things he hadn't begun to uncover during their short dinner last night?

Crossing her arms, Juliet met his gaze. "We should stay here, by the fire. If someone comes, they might put it out and leave, never realizing there are captives in the house."

He bit back a groan. Of course she would still be concerned about rescue, and unless he clued her in, she'd continue to be. But he couldn't tell her yet, not until he figured out what he wanted to do.

Such was the problem with deception. One small omission became many big lies.

"Fine, then I'll make us something and bring it down. We'll have a picnic on the beach."

She eyed him. "You can't cook."

"I'm not talking about a four-course meal complete with soup and appetizers. Will a sandwich work for your delicate palate?"

"Sure." With a small smile, she plopped down onto a large rock. "I'll be waiting."

Angry—and not entirely sure at whom—Finn slapped peanut butter and jelly on wheat bread and wrapped the sandwiches in napkins. This whole situation grated on him. Food was not going to soften the rock or the hard place he was smack in the middle of.

A quick search revealed a tray worthy of balancing a couple of water glasses down a steep flight of stairs, and he was back by the fire in ten minutes. With a less-than-perfect solution to his screaming conscience.

"Eat your sandwich, and then we'll start fires all around the perimeter of the island," he advised her. "I'm pretty sure this is Île de Etienne. If anyone with half a brain is paying attention, several fires will be cause for investigation."

He'd forgotten how Juliet constantly challenged him to be better, smarter, faster. In the past year, he'd floundered without her influence, something he'd only recently recognized. The blondes should have been a clue.

Eyebrows raised, Juliet gulped water from her glass and swallowed. "That's a great idea. Thanks for the sandwich."

Finn nodded and shoved his own sandwich in his mouth. The faster he finished, the faster they could get off this island—because no one said he had to wait around for his father to come get them. He could seek rescue on his own. Then he wouldn't be catering to the king's mad plan, but neither did he have to tell Juliet about it and risk damaging relations with her family further.

In the meantime, if they could find a way to spend time together without fighting, which was doubtful, marriage might seem like more of a possibility.

Finn and Juliet clambered up the stairs to the patio and threw as many wooden objects to the beach below as they could pick up. Alexander could bill their father for the damages as far as Finn was concerned.

The cliff went halfway around the island's perimeter and gradually sloped to sea level on the side facing south toward Africa, but they agreed their odds were best suited to fires along the shore closer to Delamer. Deep-water fishermen and cargo boats would pass by in the morning, and if the fires along the Delamer side didn't generate interest, they'd focus efforts to the south tomorrow.

The first patio chair burned a few yards from the stairs. Broken pieces of the rest of the patio set littered the shoreline beyond it. They rounded the fire and began spreading out piles of wood along the northern shore. The process was effortless. No speech required. She seemed to read his mind, leaning the boards into a cone shape, then stepping back so he could light it.

Finn had a strange sense of déjà vu or the feeling that the past year had been a horrible nightmare he'd woken from, sighing in relief because he and Juliet were together and still in love. Still happy.

At the same time, the pain of her betrayal rode in his chest, right where his heart was supposed to be. The protest had happened. They weren't together.

It was that push-pull paradox he didn't enjoy.

Juliet's hair had blown loose from the messy knot long ago and her cheeks had turned bright pink under the afternoon sun. She'd never say a word, but he'd bet her feet were cut and bloody too.

That was how she challenged him—with silent strength

he couldn't help but admire. Couldn't help but strive to match.

"Let me finish setting these fires. Why don't you go back to the house?" he suggested after they torched the third patio chair.

"What for?" She tossed a glance over her shoulder, already off to the next pile of wood—a side table.

"So you can rest. Take a long, hot bath. I'm sure you can find some jazz music to play in the bathroom." He followed her and cut to the chase. "You're getting sunburned and it doesn't take two people to set these small fires. Don't worry. If someone comes, I'll make sure they don't leave without you."

She halted in her tracks and they nearly collided. His arms came up to steady her, but she spun, eyes bright and searching. "You remember that I like to listen to music while I'm taking a bath?"

The sheer hopefulness in her tone uncoupled something in his chest, and the caustic scent of smoke sharpened a sudden memory of roasting marshmallows in the fireplace of his living room one evening when they'd opted not to brave the paparazzi.

"I remember everything about you."

The way she'd looked in the firelight that night. The way she'd felt in his arms when he'd made love to her right there on the floor. How he hadn't cared about anything but being with her; the obligations of his position, job, family—everything—eliminated for a blissful few hours.

He wanted that back. Wanted to forget all about the scandal for a while and indulge in the paradise around them. The paradise of neutral ground, no hurt, no past. The paradise of Juliet.

Marriage might be off the table, but maybe romance wasn't.

Her breathing changed, ever so slightly, and a hint of hunger bled into her expression. As if she'd read his thoughts. The throb of awareness spread, coiling through him.

As if she hated the separation between them as much as he did, she swayed into his space. Their lips played at meeting, hovering in hesitation. Then he closed the gap, taking her mouth firmly.

She flooded him, drenching him with need. Hands to her jaw, he angled her head, deepening the kiss, tasting the fire of her mouth. She moaned under him, building the pressure of sheer want in his system.

He slid a palm down her spine to cup her sweet rear, molding her body to his as he hiked that sexy yellow dress up so he could feel her bare skin. Like satin. He groaned and blindly went for the hem to remove the dress completely. Fingers ready to whip it off, he paused to give her a chance to stop him, seeking an answer to his unvoiced question.

With the scent of the sea, of fire and of Juliet engulfing his senses, he prayed the answer would be yes.

The weight and pressure of Finn's amazing lips on hers dissolved Juliet's knees. Never at a loss, he tightened his arms around her, supporting her against his body. *More, more, more.*

All the anxiety and fear she'd carried around since awakening in a strange bed in a strange place vanished. Finn was here, with her. Nothing mattered except losing herself in the sensations of a sea breeze and him. It was very welcome. Effortless, as it had always been between them.

No other man had ever made her feel as this one did, as if a tide of power had swept through her. Her body electrified as his energy zipped into her very blood.

Her dress bunched up at her waist and his fingers teased her flesh, brushing against her thighs, then her stomach. Yes. She wanted his hands everywhere.

As the kiss drew out, her heart soared.

And then plummeted.

She couldn't let him affect her this way. This wasn't an opportunity for a second chance. She'd tried at dinner last night and it hadn't worked.

No emotions. Ruthless determination.

Breaking loose—with incredible effort—she shook her head and pulled her dress back in place. "Um, we have to…"

What? The man scrambled her brains like a double heatstroke. The cuts on her feet weren't even as painful after Finn's mouth had numbed all her extremities. No more kissing. Or other stuff. It was too mind-altering.

He let her go and jerked his head toward the house, his expression blank. "Go inside. I'll finish here."

How very Finn-like to turn bossy when she didn't respond to his original suggestion. "I'm not taking a bath when I could be putting effort toward rescue."

His huff of frustration nearly made her smile. "Then go back to the house and see if you can get on the internet through the TV. I'm pretty sure I saw a video game console too. Try both."

"Aye, aye, Lieutenant." She gave him a saucy salute to hide her relief at the perfect excuse to remove herself from his overwhelming presence. Before she kissed him again.

She had to keep her wits about her and keep focused on escape, not her humming girl parts and desperately lonely soul.

She left him on the beach and limped up the stairs to the house, her mind turning over the kiss.

One minute they were setting fires, and the next she couldn't have stepped away from him at gunpoint. They'd both agreed in the car after dinner that they didn't make sense together. Somehow, she'd given him the wrong signals. Or they'd both been caught up in the heat of the moment, like two survivors in a disaster movie, inexplicably drawn to each other over shared circumstances.

Either way, it didn't matter. If it hadn't been for the kidnapping, she'd never have seen Finn again. Being held captive together didn't change facts. She could never marry him solely to promote her agenda. It would be too painful, too difficult.

And when he kissed her, she forgot all that.

She had to get off this island and away from him. It was best for them both.

The TV wasn't the kind with an internet connection, but it did have satellite cable service, offering more than three hundred channels, including all the premium movie ones. Quickly, she cued up a news channel to see how much coverage their disappearance was receiving.

After fifteen minutes of zero mentions of the missing Prince of Delamer, Juliet gave up. No one realized they'd been kidnapped yet. What kind of kidnappers waited so long to make their demands?

The credenza did indeed house a Wii console on the bottom shelf, tucked way in the back. Only Finn's sharp helicopter-pilot eyesight could have spotted it.

She hit the power button, but despite many attempts, the console couldn't connect to the internet. No service, likely. The kidnappers had been quite thorough. Absently, she flipped through the hundred or so games lining the shelf next to the console, hard-pressed to think of a title not present and accounted for.

They certainly wouldn't suffer from boredom here in this gilded cage.

Heaving a sigh, she turned off the electronics and spent several minutes opening cabinets and drawers looking for a laptop or cell phone or *something* that could be used to contact help.

The sliding glass door to the patio opened and shut, announcing Finn's return.

"Shouldn't one of us stay on the beach in case someone comes?" she asked with raised eyebrows. "I'll go back down if you don't want to."

She definitely didn't need to be in the same room with him, not while he looked all deliciously windblown and wild from being out in the elements.

His jaw tightened as he pushed his rolled sleeves up over his elbows. "It's late. I doubt there are many boaters out on the water. If one of the guys is doing my rounds, he'll land on the south side of the island to investigate. The sound of a helicopter would be hard to miss. I think it's okay to be in the house."

There was no argument for that. Her feet could use a break anyway.

Gingerly, she crossed to the couch and plopped down to contemplate. "I guess we should think about dinner."

"A shower wouldn't be out of line either."

"Are you suggesting I need one?" she teased, and nearly bit her tongue.

It came so automatically to joke around with Finn, when really, there was nothing funny about being kidnapped. Nothing funny about being stuck on a small island with him when things were so impossible between them.

His smile did nothing to ease her consternation. "*I* need the shower. But if you want to join me, I'd be okay with that."

Accompanied by an exaggerated eyebrow waggle, the invitation was clearly not intended to be taken seriously, but of course now she was thinking about Finn's unclothed body, water sluicing down his sinewy muscles as he soaped himself.

"Uh…" She shut her eyes for a blink. It didn't help. Images danced across her mind's eye, growing increasingly erotic. "Thanks. I'm good."

He chuckled as if he'd guessed the direction of her thoughts. "I'm taking the bedroom at the end of the hall. You can have the one where you woke up. See you in a few."

Moments after he blew from the room, water hummed through the pipes in the walls. *I will not think about Finn naked. I will not think about Finn naked,* she chanted silently as she heaved off the couch to see about dinner.

Naked was actually better than thinking of him fully clothed and gazing at her with his heart in his eyes. She missed that far more than sex.

Listlessly, she rooted around in the refrigerator and then the pantry, but inspiration did not strike. She'd spent two months enduring hours upon hours of wife training under Elise's and Dannie's expert hands, including many sessions in the kitchen. Proper wives learned far more than how to cook, Elise had explained. They knew ingredients, how to pair food and wine, the true cost of a meal...even if they had professional chefs or the funds to eat out regularly. Otherwise, lack of knowledge gave caterers a license to rob you blind, or the charity fund-raiser you helmed ended up way over budget.

Surely some of the lessons had stuck. After all, the entire time, Juliet had assumed she'd be matched with an American businessman, as Dannie had been. She'd paid close attention, she really had.

Instead of trying to pull information from her brain that clearly wasn't there, she spent far too long searching for a cookbook. Zilch. The gourmet kitchen with its stainless steel appliances and stone countertops either typically accommodated a chef who knew what she was doing or it was strictly for show.

Chicken breast. That seemed easy enough to pop in the oven and cook at...some temperature. When in America, the conversion between Fahrenheit and Celsius had confused her, and now here she was cooking in Europe with an oven using Celsius after all. It was enough to drive her to drink.

Well, that sounded like a plan. She hunted for the wine cellar, and sure enough, it was off the kitchen and fully stocked with labels even she could tell were pricey and rare. The cool stone walls held the chill, promising perfectly temperate wine. With no small amount of glee, she plucked an aged Bordeaux from the rack and hoped the kidnappers had a stroke when they realized the thirty-year-old bottle was gone.

Back at the maddening stove, but fortified with a full glass of the deep red wine, she hummed as she plunked chicken into a dish with one hand and drank with the other.

"Now there's a sight. I do believe that's a happy tune you're humming."

She glanced over her shoulder. Finn lounged at the kitchen entrance, one shoulder against the wall, watching her. His dark hair was still damp and he wore a pair of jeans with a navy T-shirt, which fit as if they'd been custom made for his lanky frame.

"The kidnappers brought your luggage?" She perked up. Half a glass of wine had already gone a long way toward improving her mood, but clean clothes would be a very nice bonus indeed. "Did they bring mine?"

Her sunny yellow dress had become more the shade of ten-year-old linoleum, and a long brown streak of something she'd rather not identify marred the skirt.

His high-watt smile could have baked the chicken by itself. "Afraid not. I found these clothes in the closet of my bedroom. There were some girl outfits too, so I put one on your bed for you. What are you making?"

"Chicken."

After a long pause, his eyebrows rose. "And what else?"

"There has to be more? What's wrong with just chicken?"

"Nothing's wrong with just chicken, but I'm starving. What about some bread or…" He rummaged around in the refrigerator and held up a head of romaine. "A salad?"

"Feel free to contribute whatever you like to the meal. Have some wine," she offered magnanimously. "It's a Bordeaux. Might as well take advantage of our kidnappers' hospitality."

"Don't mind if I do. Alexander's always championing the merits of that label. Let's see what all the fuss is about." He poured himself a glass and bustled around the kitchen alongside her, throwing salad in bowls and slicing hunks from the baguette he'd pulled from the pantry.

Juliet pretended not to watch but *oh, my God,* what was it about a man in the kitchen that was so sexy? Or maybe it was just *this* man, with his fluid grace and his gorgeous, muscled butt that his borrowed jeans showcased as if they'd been stitched together deliberately to induce drool.

The oven timer dinged, startling her out of an X-rated fantasy starring the tabletop, her dress around her waist and Finn's jeans on the floor.

Gah, wasn't she supposed to be *not* thinking about him naked?

Quickly, before he noticed naughty guilt plastered all over her face, she plated everything and they sat at the breakfast nook overlooking the patio. A spectacular sunset splashed the sky to the west and nearly made dinner with the former love of her life bearable.

Finn chatted about nothing and earned major points for failing to mention the dry, tasteless lump of plain chicken on his plate. And she had the nagging thought that poultry and red wine weren't supposed to go together, which someone who regularly attended formal dinners with heads of major countries probably knew like the back of his hand. He didn't make another move or even flirt with her, and he'd helped her set the fires, despite originally hating the idea.

Maybe it wasn't so bad to be stuck here with Finn.

"This is the second night in a row we've had dinner together," she commented and wished she could take it back. Why had she brought that up? She didn't want him to think she approved of the idea.

"Yes." He gave her a long look, and the heat in it meant he'd definitely interpreted her observation the wrong way. "We used to eat together all the time."

"Well, hopefully this is the last time." She cringed. "I don't mean because you're such a horrible dinner companion. But because I hope we're rescued soon."

"I knew what you meant." He stuck a bite in his mouth and chewed thoughtfully. "Once we're home, are you planning to stick around?"

"I haven't really thought that far ahead."

"You could ask Elise for a different match." His smile flattened and he put his fork down in favor of drinking deeply from his wineglass. "If you still wanted to find an American husband."

"I don't."

It was a bit of a shock, but she recognized it as truth, despite not having consciously made any decision of the sort. Her flight from Delamer had been driven by Finn's false engagement announcement. Even if it hadn't been, she'd taken the coward's way out, and that didn't sit well with her anymore.

She rushed on lest he think *he* had something to do with her decision.

"Being back here...I can't leave Delamer again. But I don't have a job, or a place to live."

He shrugged. "That's easily rectified. The new school is short on qualified teachers, and I'm pretty sure I could lean on a few people to find you an apartment."

"Why would you do that?"

Because he thought she was on board with a second chance? That kiss on the beach had led him down the wrong path.

But it hadn't meant anything. The man was a good kisser. *That's* why she couldn't quite put it out of her mind.

"Don't sound so suspicious. I saw your face on the beach. I know what the water means to you. Frankly, I was shocked you'd leave in the first place." He stared out at the sunset for a long moment. "I talked my father into building that new school. For you."

Her wineglass bobbled, nearly spilling the contents, but she caught it with only a few splattered drops sacrificed to her clumsiness. "What? You did not. The existing school was overcrowded. Everyone knows that."

She'd had thirty students in her class last year and mourned letting them go on to the next grade without having given each of them more attention. The new school had been on everyone's mind. Tourism received the majority of the government's consideration at budget time, as it should, since foreign dollars filled the coffers.

"Yes, but it's been overcrowded for a long time with little action. How do you think the powers that be became convinced a new school was critical for the future of Delamer?"

The ribbon-cutting picture of Finn and the little girl sprang into her mind. Prince Alain had cut the ribbon because he'd made the school possible. When she stumbled over the picture, she'd always been too quick to click away the painful reminders to read any of the articles. "You never said anything. I've been complaining about the size of the classes since we first met."

His gaze captured hers, and she couldn't tear her heart away from the depths of his clear blue eyes.

"It was a surprise. I wanted to be sure it was a go before I mentioned it. They'd just broken ground when we split up."

"I don't...but that means..." Her brain and tongue seemed to be operating independently of each other, and a deep breath didn't help. "The king was opposed and you talked him into it?"

"Not opposed. You know how expensive it is to build in Delamer, when all the materials have to be imported. A school wasn't a top priority. I helped him see it should be.

With all the ammunition you gave me over our dozens of conversations about it, it was pretty easy to do."

"You did that for me?" she whispered.

"For you. And for my people. If I didn't think it was necessary, I wouldn't have supported the idea. But Delamer needs educated children who will grow up and become productive members of society. Who will help us compete in a global marketplace with ever-increasing opportunities. We have to start now if Delamer hopes to stay relevant."

She'd never said any of that. Her chief concern had been doing her job and ensuring the children had the best possible environment to learn. He'd drawn his own conclusions, creating a refined, big-picture angle that someone in her position wouldn't have considered.

But he had. Because of his role in the ruling family, he had a different perspective and a greater scope of concern than simply an overcrowded building.

Her head went a little fuzzy. Finn had conspired with the king to solve a problem she'd expressed.

But not the one she'd implored him to take to his father.

She braced for the familiar rush of anger—but it wasn't as harsh as normal.

How could she be mad at Finn? Together, they'd achieved something worthwhile. Of course, she hadn't been an active participant, but what if she was? How much more could they accomplish?

Clearly Finn had been listening to her and had no problem championing a cause once he bought into it. For some reason, he hadn't bought into her impassioned pleas for military reform. Why not?

But to ask might mean answers she didn't like. No reason he could give would make more sense than lifting the mandatory military service law. It couldn't. To believe in his reasons would be a betrayal of Bernard's memory, and that she could never do.

Deep down, she secretly wondered if her brother's death

was her fault. In a family of six children, it had fallen to Juliet, as the oldest, to help with the others. She'd spent so much time with her brother—but she obviously hadn't taught him well enough how to stay safe.

Her parents grieved the loss of their only son, probably more than she could ever imagine. They'd depended on her to ensure the same end didn't happen to another family.

The look on their faces when she told them Finn refused to budge…it had ravaged her. And after losing Bernard and then Finn, she'd have sworn she had nothing left to ravage.

Nothing could possibly fix that except taking this second chance to fulfill the quest her parents expected of her. Somehow, Finn must be persuaded to eliminate the mandatory service law in Bernard's honor. Finn's reasons for not doing so initially were completely irrelevant.

Not even if those reasons led her back into Finn's arms.

<u>Six</u>

The morning dawned with no more progress toward rescue or romance.

Not that Finn had expected much of either. But it was hard to tell his fully alert and female-starved body that yes, Juliet was sleeping in the same house, but Atlantis might rise from its watery grave before she visited his bedroom in the middle of the night.

Finn groaned and rolled over in the huge, lonely bed.

That kiss haunted his dreams. The feel of her flesh, the slide of her tongue.

Dinner last night had been torturous, especially after he'd told Juliet about building the school for her. The look on her face had affected him far more than he'd expected. More than he'd been prepared for.

He'd been about to suggest taking the rest of the wine out on the deck in hopes the evening might take a more passionate turn. But she'd closed off and excused herself for the evening.

"Good morning," Finn called cheerfully from his doorway as Juliet emerged from her bedroom. She had circles
under her eyes and appeared to have slept as poorly as he
had.

Because she'd been lying awake aching in kind but was
too stubborn to admit she wanted him? Because she did
want him, regardless of what had made her pull away. No
one could kiss a man as she had and not mean it.

"It's morning. That's about all I can say about it," she
grumbled before brightening slightly. "At least I got to take
a hot shower. Thanks for the clothes."

The light sweater and pants were a little big, but she
wore them with panache. Portia's taste ran to the conser-
vative side, but then she was the crown princess and constantly under scrutiny.

"Let's eat breakfast," he said. "And then check out the
south side of the island. I have an idea for another way to
get someone's attention, but I have to see if it'll work."

"That sounds promising. And mysterious. I can't wait."

Juliet scored a couple of bagels from the pantry and
spread them with jam. Finn brewed coffee, ignoring Alexander's lame Colombian brand for the dark roast Finnish
label he'd found in the back of the pantry. They took their
booty and some slices of cantaloupe outside to the patio,
where a gentle breeze from the sea teased Juliet's hair and
made him smile. Early-morning sunshine washed the view
of Delamer in a silvery cloak and it was so achingly gorgeous, he hardly noticed the missing chairs, gladly sitting
on the hard stone to eat.

Finn wanted his own island. Once they got home, he'd
see about buying one. His future bride, whoever she was,
might like a lover's retreat. Except he couldn't get the image
of Juliet out of his mind, standing on the deck with hair
falling out of a knot, melding with the background like a
gorgeous sea creature too transcendent to catch.

The bite of bagel in his mouth wouldn't go down past the sudden lump in his throat.

Once he finally swallowed, he croaked, "Finished?"

He certainly was.

She held up her mug. "Yeah, if I can take the rest of this to go. I didn't realize how weak and boring American coffee is." She moaned a little in appreciation of the strong version in her cup. "What's the plan? More fires?"

That moan rippled through his still-alert lower half, which hadn't fully recovered from the night alone.

He shook his head. "Rocks. If we can find enough, we can spell out HELP or something that can be seen from the air. If the guys swing out to patrol the shipping lanes, someone will see it. The sooner we get it done, the better."

"Brilliant."

She disappeared into the house and reappeared with a travel mug. She'd also donned a pair of Portia's Timberlands, no doubt in anticipation of tramping along the south side of the island. "We still haven't made the news yet, by the way. Your HELP sign is a good plan since it doesn't even seem like anyone knows we're missing."

He should tell her the truth. But how could he without jeopardizing everything? If rescue came soon, he'd be off the hook.

They set off and soon had a pile of loose rocks from the perimeter of the island. As with the fires, they worked together seamlessly, but this time, Finn opted not to remain silent as they placed the stones in long lines.

"What if you didn't go back to teaching?" he threw out, picking up the threads of last night's conversation. "Could you be happy in some other job?"

Like Princess Juliet.

Where had that thought come from? He frowned. Still thinking about Juliet out on the deck, obviously, and how unhappy his father would be when Finn came home without having proposed to Juliet and without changing her mind.

"I'm sure I could find something I'd be good at besides that." She paused, a rock in each hand.

"What about something you'd like? As opposed to something you'd be good at." It was an interesting distinction, one he'd bet she hadn't consciously made.

With the "H" complete, he moved over to start laying the first branch of the "E." Juliet dropped her two rocks into place after his, clacking them together haphazardly.

"Ow!" She jerked her hand back and examined it.

"Are you okay?"

"Stupid fake fingernails." She frowned at the thin, bloody line splitting her index fingernail into two halves. "One got caught between the rocks and cracked down to the quick. I didn't even know that could happen. Usually I break them off."

"Why have them in the first place then?"

She shrugged and dropped her hand, the nail forgotten even though it had to hurt. "Such is the way of females, I'm told. We're supposed to be polished and put together."

"You don't have to have fingernails to be attractive, you know," he said.

"I know. You never cared about me being ladylike, which I always appreciated. That's why Elise's computer matched us, I suppose."

Actually, they'd been matched because they shared similar beliefs and moral compasses. Which was why he understood that she'd been upset and irrational when her brother died. If their positions were reversed and Alexander had been the one to walk into a live electrical field, Finn would be a wreck.

Polish mattered little in the grand scheme of things, but if he could convince her how wrong she'd been to take the position she had, they'd be dealing with a whole new set of dynamics.

Romance *and* marriage could be on the table.

Time healed wounds and afforded a different perspective. Maybe now she could see facts rationally. Could he really let go of the opportunity to feel her out?

Then he could truthfully tell his father he'd tried.

"You've never been out on the deck of the *Aurélien*," he said casually.

"No." She knelt carefully in the bare dirt where they were working, and placed the next rock with deliberate care, her back to Finn.

And that was the extent of her reaction to his abrupt subject change.

The stiffness of her spine and jerkiness of her movements told him she'd recognized the name of the ship where her brother had taken his last breath.

He almost backed off. His usual method of operation. Why should he have to spell out something she should already know?

But this was too important to stay in his comfort zone.

He sat down next to her and rearranged the already perfectly placed rocks. "It's an air defense frigate. I'm sure you've seen it from shore. Plenty of anti-aircraft guns and missile launchers and general busyness on deck. Extremely complicated equipment and lots of confusing levels."

"Yeah. I've seen it."

She wasn't going to make this easy, which was partly why he'd never talked about this before.

"They go over safety protocol all the time." He'd chosen his words carefully, but some things needed to be said without censor. "It's the responsibility of each private to understand the rules and follow them."

"Are you about to suggest that Bernard didn't?" she cut in, her tone strident.

"I wasn't there," he said as gently as possible. "But the reports were pretty conclusive. They interviewed all the shipmen aboard at the time. You can't go into the electrical rooms without proper protection."

Her head dropped as if too heavy for her neck to support.

"He shouldn't have been on that ship in the first place." She met Finn's gaze, and her ravaged expression tore through him. "He wanted to be in the coast guard. Like you. He worshipped you. Couldn't say enough about your flying skills or how heroically you rescued a swimmer."

That was a double spike to the gut. Finn wasn't a hero, or someone worthy of worshipping.

"The path to the coast guard is three years of mandatory military service," he said brusquely. "I did it too. I hated every second of being a shipman, but Juliet, half of Delamer borders the water. Our naval presence is paramount, and that's where we need men. Our population is so miniscule. How else would we get people on those boats?"

"Do you think the word *help* is enough or should we tack on an exclamation point?" She stood and gathered another pile of rocks with exaggerated movements.

He struggled with whether to drop it or not. Honestly, the subject was a little raw for him too. He'd liked Bernard. Finn could easily imagine having him around on a guy's fishing weekend or eventually becoming the boy's mentor, if he'd gone the coast guard route after serving his three years.

Juliet's broken half sob decided it for him.

Finn yanked her into his arms and snuggled her wet face against his neck. She snuffled for a moment, then her arms clasped him in turn. Her tears flowed unapologetically onto his shoulder, but he didn't care.

He held her, hurting along with her. "Bernard was a great kid. I miss him too."

"I just want to reverse time, you know?" she whispered. "Make it not have happened."

"I know." He breathed in the scent of her hair and the sea and lost a tear or two, as well. "It was a tragedy. But we have to move on, sweetheart."

She stepped out of his arms, and the rush of cool air

burned his Juliet-warmed skin. Obviously that had been the wrong thing to say.

"Move on. Good idea. This is done." She slid a finger under her wet lashes and then waved at the HELP sign stretching across the dirt before them. "You wait here for one of your buddies to make rounds. I'm going to the north side of the island to see if any boats are sailing from the marina to one of the other islands. Maybe I can flag one down."

This time, he let the matter drop. He watched her walk away and cursed.

Somehow, the dynamic between them had grown more complicated. And he had a feeling the longer they stayed on this island together, the worse it would become.

Juliet escaped and willed herself to stop crying. It wasn't working so far.

For brief odd moments, she'd experienced peace while placing stones with Finn, as if things had never become so mucked up. As if they were working together, teasing each other and laughing, then they'd look up and be finished without realizing any time had passed.

Then he'd ruined it.

Why did Finn have to pick at her wounds like that? And then be so understanding and comfortable to cry on? His shoulder was always on offer, always strong, and she'd missed it.

But then, she'd never really had it, not after Bernard died. The reminder was brutal.

The ache in her chest wouldn't ease, no matter how many deep breaths she took or how many times she counted to one hundred. Usually counting put her in a Zen-like state and cleared her mind. Not today.

She had to get away from Finn permanently. He was screwing with her sense of well-being.

"Come on, just one boat," she muttered.

A bright yellow catamaran skipped over the water about two hundred yards off the Delamer marina but no one on board would notice a lone woman waving at them from the shore of an island that was merely a smear on their horizon.

How long would she have to wait for a boat to come close enough to the island?

"I brought you an umbrella from the house."

She whirled. Finn stood behind her, umbrella opened and extended. Summer was typically the dry season in the Mediterranean. Only Finn would have thought to look for an umbrella. Only Finn would think of shielding her from the sun while she stood here waiting for a miracle rescue.

"I didn't hear you come down the stairs," she said.

"You seemed pretty intent on your self-appointed task. Sorry if I scared you."

She shook her head and took the offered shade. "Thanks."

Finn glanced out over the water. "It's a beautiful morning, isn—"

"I thought you were going to wait on the other side of the island."

They weren't doing this casual-conversation thing anymore. She couldn't take it. Not while it still felt as if an elephant was sitting on her chest.

If only he hadn't brought up Bernard. But he had and now it was alive again between them, hanging in that space where their love for each other used to be.

Surprise flitting through his gaze, Finn stared at her. "I can hear a helicopter on the north side as easily as I can hear one on the south. Thought I'd make sure you were okay."

"What, like I can't take care of myself?"

"No, like because you were crying," he corrected mildly. "I didn't mean to upset you."

"I'm fine." Since that clearly wasn't true, she offered the catch-all, noncommittal, leave-me-alone excuse. "Tired. Being kidnapped takes it out of me."

"Yeah, and the subject material too, apparently. Was it better to not talk about it?"

"I don't know."

Sometimes she *did* want to talk about it, and who better understood the anguish she'd endured than Finn? He knew her family, knew her history of helping raise Bernard, knew she was the oldest Villere child in a family of six and how her sense of responsibility had shaped her path.

He knew *her,* through and through. Which was why it hurt so much to be separated.

"What would talking about it solve?"

He shrugged. "Help ease the grief. It's something I didn't get a chance to do the first time. I want to be there for you. Let me."

The idea sprouted inside her, growing and twining through her frozen insides until she could hardly bite back the *yes.*

That had been the hardest part of the past year, that she couldn't turn to Finn during one of the worst periods of her life. She'd spent a lot of time with her parents, of course, but they had each other. Her sisters were understandably lost in their own grieving process, and none of them had helped raise Bernard. They'd lost a brother they loved, but it wasn't the same as losing a boy you'd helped shape and teach.

It wasn't the same as blaming yourself for not teaching him well enough. And then blaming yourself for exposing a sweet, impressionable kid to a man like Finn, worthy of hero-worship, worthy of inspiring Bernard to follow in his footsteps.

But then, no one could understand that. Not even Finn.

And still…the Finn-shaped hole inside yearned to be filled by the man within touching distance, to let him make good on that promise to be there for her. It had always been the two of them, together forever.

Two hearts being as one.

She stepped back, clutching the umbrella with both hands. Finn couldn't grant her absolution. He couldn't even give her the unconditional support she'd desperately hoped for. And then he'd tried to act as if Bernard was to blame for not following the rules.

Latching on to that as a shield against the firestorm of angst raging through her chest, she refused to fall into Finn's arms this time. "It's too late to be there for me. Just like it's too late for us. We're over and so is this conversation."

Finn's mouth clamped into a hard line. Finally, she'd gotten through to him.

If she could only get him to understand it was his stubbornness that stood in their way. All he had to do was lose it and then take her side against his father.

If he did, she was convinced that would be the key to healing. That one thing would allow her to stop blaming herself.

But that was never going to happen.

She sniffed and cleared her throat. "We're short a helicopter patrol and clearly we're too far out to be seen by any boats coming from the marina. The only way off this island is to swim. So that's what I'm doing."

His gaze cut to the sea lapping at the rocky coastline behind her. "Swim where?"

"To shore." She nodded toward the south bank of Saint Tropez. "It's not more than two miles if I head to the French side."

"You've never swam a stretch like that in your life. What makes you think you can do it now?" His tone was deceptively even, but she heard the condescension underneath. He thought she was too weak and too female.

"I can swim two miles. I've done it lots of times." She'd have that drive to succeed in her favor too, born of desperation to get out of this situation at all costs.

"There's a big difference between doing it in shallow

water where we sail and doing it from Île de Etienne to Saint Tropez." He gripped her shoulders earnestly. "Juliet, this is a rocky area. The boating lanes were cleared of submerged obstacles, so I could see you making the mistake of thinking the whole area's clear. It's not. You're talking about swimming in a straight line across open water."

The genuine concern on his face nearly had her second-guessing the plan. But what choice did they have? They were captives and people were undoubtedly worried about them by now.

"I'll be careful."

"It's not a matter of being careful." He shifted from foot to foot, and forked a restless hand through his dark hair. "I rescue people from these waters all the time. You know the number one reason they can't swim to shore on their own? Because they misjudged their strength against the current."

"You don't think I can make it."

She wanted to hear him admit flat out that his concern was about her abilities, not the water she'd been on or in for most of her life.

"This is not about you. It's about being safe and not taking chances. If nothing else, consider that you might get hit by a boat."

The eye roll might have come across a little exaggerated. But who could blame her? "The lack of boats is one of our current problems. At least if I got run over, the boat would notice me."

"You're being flip about this and it's not the kind of thing to be flip about. That's how people die."

The harsh, deep lines of his face hit her all of a sudden. He was worried about her dying.

And then it truly would be too late.

Her heart twisted painfully and she almost reached out to reassure him. Or maybe for another reason, one she could barely acknowledge.

She didn't want it to be too late.

She wanted to find a way to be with Finn again. To recapture the easiness of being in love, the shared smiles, the lazy afternoons, the comfort. To forget about what had happened and move forward.

Her pulse thumped erratically with the realization, scaring her. It was an impossible dream because she *couldn't* forget. They were like two battering rams, pushing each other with all their might but neither giving ground. Look what a disaster their date back in Dallas had become.

Even *thinking* about being with Finn again meant she had to get away from him before she did something she couldn't take back. Something she'd regret.

The umbrella dropped from her shaking fingers.

"Staying here isn't an option."

She jammed her hands down on her hips to hide her consternation. The fact that his concerns were valid was irrelevant.

"We've tried fires. We've tried your HELP sign. No one's come yet and the boats are too far away. We have to try something else."

She twisted her hair up in a knot and kicked off her shoes, but he grabbed her hand before she could flee into the water. "Wait. We're safe here. There's no danger from the kidnappers. They'd have come back by now if they were going to. We have plenty to eat. Why don't we pretend we're on holiday and relax for a few days?"

His earnest blue eyes bored into hers, pleading for her to reconsider. He was serious. "You're insane. We're prisoners. The luxuriousness of the cage doesn't change that. I can't stay here and pretend it's okay that we were kidnapped. I'll send someone for you as soon as I can."

"Juliet, there's something you need to know." Finn squeezed her hand, tight, preventing her from pulling away. "You don't have to swim anywhere because…my father is behind this."

"Behind what?" Her gaze flitted over his dark expression. Suddenly it all came together and she yanked her hand out of his grasp. "The *kidnapping?* Your father kidnapped us?"

Sighing, he laced his fingers together behind his neck, as if his head needed help staying upright. "Yeah."

Her stomach rolled. The king hired those men in the van, who had drugged both her and Finn, then left them here. "Wait a minute. You knew your father had us kidnapped? Since when?"

His jaw worked and then squared. "Since the first day. There was a note in my pocket."

He'd known the whole time and hadn't bothered to tell her. Where was this note anyway?

She cursed. "We've been running around trying to get rescued and setting fires and your father *knew* we were trapped here. He dumped us on this island on purpose. Why in the world would he do something so horrible to his own son? To me?"

"It's complicated." Finn paused and she nearly grabbed his shoulders to shake the rest out of him. "He saw the picture of us together at Elise's party and it snowballed from there."

"So this is an attempt to keep us out of the press." The *nerve* of King Laurent. Apparently a crown gave him license to do whatever he wanted. "Can't have any photos floating around of his precious son by the side of that extremist Villere girl."

"That's not the issue, Juliet. Be quiet for five seconds and listen."

That pushed her over the edge.

"Stop being so bossy! You've known about this all along. You had your chance to talk. Now it's my turn." For once, he clamped his mouth closed and crossed his arms, allowing her to vent every ounce of frustration. "How you sprang from the loins of such a coldblooded man as the king, I'll never understand. He put us in danger, just like he put Bernard in danger, and I'm tired of neither you nor your father seeing the problem. And I'm not going to sit around and wait for him to make the next move."

With that parting shot, she sprinted into the water.

The chill of it stole her breath. The summer was too young to have warmed the temperature, and she hated to admit it was an obstacle she hadn't even considered.

Well, it didn't matter. She could do it. She had to, if for no other reason than to prove to King Laurent that he didn't control her.

Stroking rhythmically, she pulled away from the island slowly, opting to conserve her energy for the middle stretch.

Breathe. Stroke. Breathe, stroke.

It was *so cold*.

She risked a glance around, and saw she'd hardly traveled more than three hundred yards. Checking her progress was a stupid thing to do. It was better not to know how far she still had to go and just swim. She'd hit the distant shore at some point. What did it matter how close she was?

A tingle in her fingers spread up her hands. Oh, no. They were going numb.

She stretched them as she stroked, hoping to increase the blood flow.

Then her side cramped.

And she sucked in a mouthful of seawater.

Coughing and holding her spasming waist, she treaded water mindlessly, frantically, praying the pain would ease as quickly as it had come on.

Water from her hair spilled into her eyes, stinging them. She backhanded the moisture away, but the second she moved her arm, the cramp in her side knifed through her anew, nearly sinking her under the surface.

The sea she loved had turned on her.

No, the sea was the same as always. Her time in America had taken its toll and she was woefully underconditioned for a swim like this. She should have been weight training and doing laps in the pool instead of learning how to balance a book on her head.

Her legs burned with the effort to keep her head above water. She wasn't going out like this, not by drowning in the Mediterranean. Any other body of water but this one, and she'd have considered giving in to the dizzying fatigue.

Gritting her teeth against the pain, she swam a couple of more yards, congratulating herself on each painstaking stroke and kick.

A wave rolled her and turned her head into the swell. Another unwelcome mouthful of seawater went down her throat.

Coughing impeded her progress once again. As soon as she started treading water, a vicious cramp lit up her abdomen, drawing her torso toward her knees involuntarily. Which were underwater.

She had to go back.

Relieved tears pricked at her stinging eyes. She could go back to the island. It didn't feel so much like giving up as survival, and that she could live with.

The decision made, she kicked in the direction of Île de Etienne and counted to five before the cramp in her side jerked her to a halt.

Water burned down her esophagus. When she coughed involuntarily, it shafted into her lungs. Death by drowning became a litany in her head, shouting its presence until she was nearly screaming *no, no, no.* But another mouthful of water contradicted that.

She wasn't going to make it.

This would be her watery grave, precisely as Finn had predicted.

Her tears of relief turned to tears of regret. So many regrets. She hadn't called her mom in a week. She'd never watch another child form his first words in English with her instruction as his guide. Her womb would never grow a child of her own.

Worst of all, she'd never have a chance to tell Finn she still loved him. Why had she clung to her anger for so long?

Just as she thought she'd black out for the last time, Finn was somehow there in the water with her, pulling her into a rescue headlock and towing her to shore.

She went limp and let herself float, desperately sucking air into her body and pushing water out. She wasn't going to die. It wasn't too late.

Seven

Finn tucked Juliet into the larger bed he'd slept in last night and put two blankets over her, cursing Alexander's inability to stock one tiny thermometer in this whole house.

Juliet's skin blazed, almost too hot to touch. She had a fever, no question. He would have liked the confirmation of how high. And whether it was climbing higher or dropping.

Stubborn woman.

Why had she tried to swim to Saint Tropez?

He knew why. She refused to believe he might be right, even about something as important as whether she could actually beat the sea he knew better than his own name. Even telling her about his father's role in the kidnapping hadn't convinced her they were safe and that escape wasn't necessary.

And that was a poor excuse designed to absolve his guilt. It didn't work.

He should have told her sooner about his father's involvement in the kidnapping. If he had, she might not have conceived of the idea of swimming across open water. If anything, his confession had pushed her into it.

No time to wallow in his mistakes. He shed his wet clothes in record time, then threw on some dry ones. Slipping beneath the sheets to lay on the other pillow, he watched her chest rise and fall, telling himself he wanted to be near in case she needed him.

It was a lie.

He couldn't physically separate himself from Juliet after nearly losing her in such a heart-stopping fashion. There on the rocky shore, he'd performed the sloppiest mouth-to-mouth resuscitation on record, but he hadn't been able to stop shaking.

Finally, she had convulsed and started breathing on her own. How he'd managed to haul her up the flight of stairs and into the house with legs the consistency of a wet noodle, he still didn't know.

He held her hand tightly underneath the covers. She was so weak, her fingers slipped from his if he let his grip go slack. Her tangled, still-wet hair draped over the pillow, and he wished he'd thought to grab a towel and dry it before settling in.

The ill-advised feelings stirred up by her unconscious state had to go. But she was so fragile and beautiful, and he couldn't stand the thought of losing her.

Time passed. An hour, then two. Juliet thrashed occasionally and then fell so still, it scared him into pressing his fingertips to a pulse point, just to be sure she hadn't taken her last breath right there in front of him.

Surely the king couldn't have envisioned his plan playing out in quite this way. Despite exhaustion, which ran deep into his bones, Finn found a bit of energy left over to be furious with his father.

Juliet was sick and they had no method of communicating with the outside world. No way of contacting a doctor, of shipping in medicine or shipping Juliet out to a hospital.

Sheer helplessness ran rampant, weighing him down more than the fatigue and concern. It hadn't been easy to swim through the island's natural eddies, then tow another person back to shore, all the while terrified Juliet had already succumbed to the hidden dangers of the sea.

Hunger forced him from the bed as the sun began to set. He dashed to the kitchen, shoved some crackers down his throat, drank two full glasses of water and dashed back to the bed to pick up his vigil where he left off.

A tug on his hand startled Finn into opening his eyes. Automatically, he glanced at the digital clock on the bedside table. Three a.m. Had he fallen asleep?

He glanced at Juliet. The dim light he'd left on in the bathroom spilled over her open eyes. She blinked at him owlishly.

"Hey," he whispered and cupped the side of her face. Still hot, but maybe not as hot as before. "How do you feel?"

She turned her cheek into his hand. Deliberately. As if she actually wanted to be closer to his touch. Then she licked her lips and swallowed a couple of times. "Like someone dropped me in a volcano."

"You have a fever. It was probably something you picked up back in America and it took this long to surface." His thumb trailed over her jaw and his lower half suddenly needed a stern lecture about Juliet's illness and the inappropriateness of being turned on by a woman too weak to respond in kind.

Too late. His body throbbed to life. Exhaustion and stress had lowered his defenses entirely too much for any sort of admonishment to be effective anyway. So now he'd suffer from unrequited sexual frustration in addition to everything else. Fantastic.

Hopefully she wouldn't notice.

"You saved me," she murmured, and the dim light perfectly showcased the tender gratitude beaming from her expression.

"Yeah. What else would I have done?"

"Let me drown. Like I deserved."

He made a face. "Right, that was going to happen."

"How…did you get there so fast? I was way offshore."

Of all the questions—of course she'd ask that one. She was the only swimmer he'd ever rescued who would have even realized the distance he'd traversed to get to her. He sighed and told her the truth, though she wasn't going to like it.

"I was following you. In the water. When you went in, I went in."

"Oh." Her eyes closed for a beat and she dragged them open with what looked like considerable effort. "You didn't think I could make it."

"No." He thought about apologizing. But he wasn't sorry he'd set off after her. Thank God he had.

"Why did you let me go?" she whispered, her voice raw.

"Because I'm not in the habit of forcing women to do things primarily," he said drily. "And also because you needed to try."

A trove of emotions traveled over her face. He couldn't begin to read them all. But he'd bet at least one of them was irritation at his lack of faith.

"That's…interesting," was all she said, and the break in her voice worried him.

"It's the middle of the night. You should be getting rest, not hashing this out. Sleep. I'll be here."

It was an unintentional echo of their earlier conversation, when he'd told her he wanted to be there for her during her grief.

"You don't have to take care of me," she muttered. "I'm the one who should be taking care of you."

"I'm not sick," he pointed out. "Next time I have a fever, I'll let you put me to bed, okay?"

Her hand squeezed his and went slack a few moments later as she drifted off.

Sleep eluded him and by dawn, Juliet hadn't moved so he risked leaving her long enough to take a much-needed shower.

Hot water flowed over his abused muscles, soothing them. He hadn't realized how much he needed a break from the uncomfortable position he'd elected to take in the bed, half hunched against the headboard. But it was the optimal spot for monitoring Juliet.

There in the confines of the enclosed shower stall, finally alone, the sheer terror he'd kept at bay loosened and bled from the center of his chest.

It nearly knocked him to his knees.

He could have lost Juliet. And only now did he realize how much he wanted this second chance his father had given him.

Somehow, he had to find a path to the other side of the huge wall between them. Not because of any advantageous marriage, but because he truly didn't think he could function for the rest of his life without her.

That was the king's ace in the hole. Finn hadn't fallen out of love with Juliet after all, and the kidnapping had brought those emotions to the surface.

What if he *could* find a way to change Juliet's heart? There was no better place or time on earth to try than while trapped together in paradise.

His own heart lurched sweetly at the thought of a future with the woman he loved by his side, all their differences resolved. Marriage. Family. A place where he could achieve some normalcy, away from the public eye.

Unfortunately, a path around that wall between them didn't exist, given that she'd seemed so eager to swim away from a perfectly good island with him on it. She hadn't even given him a chance to explain the rest of his father's plot.

That was the reality clutching his heart in its steely fingers—she didn't want him on her side of the wall. Reconciliation seemed quite impossible. No matter how badly he might now want it.

When he returned to the bedroom, she was propped up against several pillows watching TV. Some color had returned to her face, but not enough for his liking.

"Good morning," she rasped and scowled. "My throat hurts."

"I'll get you a drink, okay?"

She nodded and he fetched a glass of water from the bathroom, which she drank in two gulps. "Better."

"How do you feel?" He touched the back of his hand to her forehead. Still hot.

"Let's cut to the chase, shall we? I'm not getting out of bed for the foreseeable future. Will that make you stop hovering?"

Her bristly tone was back. "I'm not hovering."

She shot him a look and nodded to his side of the bed. "Unless you want to be known as Prince Mother Hen, sit down."

He did, gingerly. "I'm concerned about you. That's all."

"And I appreciate it, but I'm not going to break. I can't swim to Saint Tropez in my current physical condition, but I'm not so fragile that you have to be at my beck and call."

Ah, so this was about her dogged determination to prove she could do whatever she set her mind to. Admirable, but also the reason they weren't married with two kids right now.

She just couldn't admit when she was wrong.

He might have the capacity to love her, but not necessarily the fortitude.

She clicked the remote a few times and tossed it to the bed, then snuggled down into the blankets. Somehow, she'd scooted over the invisible center line, onto his side. "Did I say thank you earlier?"

TV forgotten, she blinked at him with a small smile.

Awareness rolled over him with the force of a powerful whitecap.

He waved it off, his mouth suddenly dry. "You can show your gratitude by getting well and making me a proper meal."

"I'm working on it." She lay back against the pillow. "So tired."

Her legs shifted under the covers, sliding along his until they were flush. She appeared not to notice, had probably even done it accidentally. No matter. Thick layers of fabric separated them, but his skin heated as if all the obstacles between them were gone.

Desperate to get off the bed before he did something foolish, like strip naked and slide under the covers with her, he blurted out, "Do you feel well enough for a bath?"

Her closed eyes fluttered open. "I'd like that. Will you help me?"

Bad idea, his conscience screamed, followed shortly by, *Shut up now.* "I thought you didn't want me hovering."

"It's not hovering if I ask you, silly." Her small, delicate smile blossomed into a larger one that hit him in all the right places. "My skin feels crusty. I don't think I can reach it all."

"I'll help you to the bathroom, but that's as far as I go."

She lifted a wan hand to her forehead. "I need you. Please?"

Coupled with the liquid depths of her pleading gaze, how could he say no?

He fled to the bathroom and ran warm water into the huge marble tub. For good measure, he dumped half a bottle of Portia's oriental bubble bath into the water, hoping the foam would cover enough of Juliet to allow him the possibility of getting through this with his dignity intact.

The exotic scent of sandalwood and jasmine filled the bathroom, and instantly transformed the space from utilitarian to seductive. So much for dignity. He could have plastered the walls with erotic pictures and not achieved such a sensual effect.

Because the torture wasn't already brutal enough, he flipped on the entertainment system mounted to the wall and found a jazz station on satellite radio. The heavy, sultry wail of a saxophone poured through the surround-sound system.

"Finn?" she called from the bedroom, and the sound of his name from her raspy throat spiraled the tension higher.

He shut his eyes for a beat, but it didn't fortify him nearly enough.

Clamping down on his imagination, he hustled to the bed and hustled Juliet out with nary a sidelong glance at the T-shirt he'd haphazardly pulled onto her naked body last night, in place of her drenched clothes.

The simple T-shirt hadn't seemed sexy last night. This morning, it pleaded for a man's hands to lift the hem, just a fraction, revealing all her secrets.

He groaned and turned his back. "Get in the tub. All the way in. Let me know when you're covered up by the suds."

Please take a long time.

"Ready."

"Trying to set the land speed record for bathing?" he muttered and peeked at the bathtub. Sure enough, she'd submerged neck-deep into the water, head thrown back against the tub's lip, eyes closed.

Worst nightmare and hottest fantasy rolled into one.

"Fever, fever, fever," he mumbled and tried to remember the quickest way to break one. He cursed. He should have drawn a *cold* bath—with ice cubes. Or maybe that was the cure for a raging erection. His could use an ice bath the size of Delamer.

Juliet's eyes drifted open. "I know I have a fever. I feel awful."

"I wasn't talk—never mind." Yanking the soap, shampoo and a washcloth from the cabinet beside the vanity, he parked on the edge of the tub. "Let me wash your hair, then you do the rest."

He poured out enough shampoo to wash at least four women's hair—because there was no way he'd have the stamina to do this over if he messed up—and lathered her hair as quickly as possible. "Okay, rinse."

With what looked like considerable effort, she ducked under the water and came up with her eyes closed. He put a towel into her questing fingers and was about to stand and escape when her hand covered his knee.

"Don't go," she murmured. "Scrub my back."

Dark, wet strands of hair covered the area in question, which he could not keep his eyes off of. "I thought we agreed you could do that."

"No, you issued a royal decree. Doesn't make it possible for me to lift my arms that high."

Scootching backward, she presented her bare form for his touching pleasure. Except this was supposed to be a utilitarian process, designed to wash dried seawater from her skin. Not foreplay.

He swallowed and soaped the washcloth. Maybe if he didn't actually touch her, it wouldn't be so bad.

The cloth skimmed down her spine, eliciting a small moan from deep in her throat. Heat spiraled tighter in his abdomen, traveling south whether he wanted it to or not. Body on full alert, he ached to drop the cloth and let his fingertips glide along the ridge of her shoulders instead.

A silver chain around her neck flashed in the low light, and he couldn't stop staring at the place where it met skin. The necklace was new. What did the combination of cool metal on hot flesh feel like?

One little touch. It had been so long. He could reacquaint his senses with the feel of her and wash the grit away at the same time. A practical solution and good for everyone.

But he didn't do it. And not because of the fever.

If they reconciled—*if*—he didn't want it to happen like

this, catering to his father's whims, with the possibility that Juliet might think he wanted to be with her because of her family's politics.

These extraordinary circumstances couldn't possibly create a connection that would translate into a lasting relationship. In his mind, the only real chance they had was to escape first and then see how things went back in Delamer.

If he recalled, the exact words she'd flung at him before trying for a gold medal in cross-country backstroke were, *We're over and so is this conversation.*

He swiped her back, lower, but she moaned again, crossing his eyes. Did she *have* to make that noise as if he'd palmed one of her breasts?

She whimpered and her head fell forward on her knees. "My skin is a little tender. Probably from the fever. Can you hurry?"

"Am I hurting you?" Horrified, he yanked the washcloth away, cursing under his breath.

While he'd been devolving into full-on guy mode, she'd been in pain. None of the names he called himself seemed enough.

"No, not too much. It's just…prickly."

"Do you want me to stop?"

Half of him hoped the answer was yes. The other half prayed it was no.

He missed the simple pleasure of being nothing more than a man touching a beautiful woman. Juliet gave him that. There wasn't a blonde on the planet who ever had or ever could.

She peered over her wet shoulder, eyelids lowered as if she had very naughty thoughts to shield from him. "It's okay. You can keep going."

Sure he could. No problem.

Sweat dribbled between his shoulder blades.

Why was he doing this to himself? The pain of the past year wasn't buried deep enough, the complications on top of that were rampant and she was so very, very naked. Masochism at its finest.

"Thanks," she whispered. "I'm glad you're here."

Warmth of the nonsexual, emotional variety spread through his chest. Yeah. That was why. He wanted to make her feel better, regardless of the cost to himself.

His outdated, inconvenient sense of honor really pissed him off sometimes.

"Me, too. You'd be shark bait otherwise." He swallowed all the squishy, girlie stuff and prayed her fever would break soon. So they could get off this island before he snapped.

After considerable effort, Juliet dressed in another borrowed outfit from the well-stocked closet and allowed Finn to help her to the sofa in the living room. She tucked her feet under the blanket and rested her aching head on Finn's shoulder. For all her grousing, she kind of liked letting Finn take care of her, though she'd deny it to her grave.

She made a face at the TV screen and winced at the stabbing pain through her temples. Everything hurt. Her chest. Her head. Her arms and legs—but that was probably residual muscle fatigue from her unsuccessful escape attempt.

"I'm sorry we're stuck watching this boring movie," she said.

But he couldn't be nearly as sorry as she was.

She hadn't made it to Saint Tropez. And now she was sick and Finn had been forced into caring for her after saving her life.

He'd rescued her. *After* he let her tear off into the water, knowing the odds of her actually making it to the other side were slim to none. He'd let her go anyway. Because he understood what drove her.

The wash of sheer gratitude almost soothed away the bitter taste of failure.

"It's okay. I hate that you feel so bad." His tender grin

looped through her stomach and came out a good bit lower, warming her insides. Okay, it wasn't *just* gratitude.

He'd unearthed something powerful and deep. And it cut through her in a terrible, wonderful way. Finn had been there, right when she needed him.

She hated needing anyone, let alone him. He hadn't been there before when she needed him. What if she let herself trust him and he let her down again?

But she still loved him, that much was clear. And she hated that too.

"I—" A coughing spell cut off the rest and she let it go. What could she possibly say?

I'm conflicted about how you make me feel. Thank you for rescuing me, but can you go to the other side of the island until I figure out how to not be in love with you?

Finn took her hand and held it in his lap, his attention on her, not the movie. Like old times. It kicked up a slow burn in some really delicious places. Places she'd rather he not affect, not when so many unwelcome, baffling things were swirling around in her heart.

"You don't have to talk."

His thumb smoothed over her knuckle, and the contact lit her up. Coupled with the emotional turmoil, watching a movie together sounded less and less like a good idea. But she couldn't face being alone in the bed, aching and wishing for something, or someone, to make her feel better. Someone like Finn.

He'd given her a bath, even though he clearly would have preferred not to. She didn't blame him. She'd been a little snippy on the beach and then he'd had to rescue her. She'd be mad at her too.

"I do feel like death warmed over, but I can still talk." More coughing made a complete liar out of her. Her eyes watered fiercely but not enough to hide Finn's told-you-so smirk.

Her arms were too heavy to lift, let alone smack him one. So she settled for glaring at him.

"Why don't you focus on resting instead of trying to prove me wrong?" he suggested and smoothed a strand of hair away from her face. "The sooner your fever breaks, the sooner we can regroup on the escape effort."

He sounded as exasperated about taking care of her as she felt about him having to. "Look at the bright side. We're stuck together in this beautiful house. There's no danger to worry about. We can hang out while I get better. It'll be fun."

Hang out had a much more superior ring to it than *nursing an invalid.*

His mouth quirked up charmingly. "Seems like that's what I suggested not too long before you waded out into the water."

"And here I am agreeing with you."

"If only that was the start of a long-term trend," he mumbled good-naturedly. "Since this movie is so boring, let's play something on the Wii."

That was why she'd always loved staying in when they'd been dating. Finn's creative streak never ran dry. Everything became fun or a precursor to making love. Usually both.

"Sure." She shoved all the unbidden images behind a blank wall in her mind. The last thing she needed to be thinking about was how much she missed Finn's particular brand of seduction. "As long as it's not too complicated or one of those war games with lots of blood and shooting. Oh, and no zombies. Or aliens."

"That pretty much eliminates…" He flipped through the titles. "All of them. Wait, here's *Super Mario Brothers.* That'll work."

In minutes, Finn set up the game and they began blipping through the levels, laughing as they battled over who got the power-ups. The colorful graphics and lively music infused a sense of peace over them. All their grievances faded away the further they journeyed into the fantastical world of plumbers, walking mushrooms and flying manta rays.

Though Finn and Juliet had never played this particular game together, they were a formidable team and the opposition stood no chance. When he went high, she instinctively went low. When she charged ahead into the thick of enemy territory, he followed, knocking out bad guys right and left, backing her up every step of the way.

As he had in the water yesterday.

Of course if he hadn't brought up Bernard, and then double-whammied her with his father's treachery, she might not have ever set foot in the sea. Yet, he'd been there when it counted, despite being told it was too late.

She couldn't stop thinking about it, about him and all the wonderful things that comprised his character.

It made her question everything.

"Piece of cake," she said after they'd defeated a particularly hard level.

She couldn't swim to France, but at least she could kick the pants off fictional villains. The cartoon monster on the screen fizzled as he died, and his expression made her giggle.

"I'm surprised you're enjoying this." Finn hit the icon to go to the next world. "Given that the object of the game is to rescue Princess Peach."

She scowled. "That's the object? I thought it was to get to the next level."

"The levels have to end sometime. On the last one, Mario rescues the princess from a birdcage."

"So you've played this before."

Disappointment walloped her.

Somehow, she'd built up a scenario where they were playing so well as a team because they were both focusing on the here and now instead of History. Because he really understood what lay beneath her surface.

Obviously their success was instead a product of his familiarity with the game.

"A few times with Portia." He looked away, likely feeling guilty over not having divulged this information before. "It's her favorite but I don't get asked to play very often. Only when Alexander is off doing crown prince duty."

"Figures she'd like it."

Portia was a princess through and through, as if she'd been born to the crown instead of marrying it. Juliet hadn't spent much time with the next queen of Delamer, but when she did, the gracious woman never failed to make Juliet feel gauche and as if they were lifelong friends simultaneously. It was a talent, no doubt.

"It's just a game," Finn said lightly and bumped her shoulder with his.

It was far from just a game. The whole concept encapsulated what was wrong with the world. And poked at her discomfort over the fact that she'd required rescue, as well. Because she hadn't been strong enough to save herself.

"It's sexist and stereotypical. How come Mario didn't get kidnapped?"

Finn glanced at her and did a double take at her expression. "Because Mario and Luigi are the stars. If you want to play something where a woman is the star, go get *Tomb Raider*."

"Why can't there be a setting or something that you flip that changes who gets kidnapped?" She warmed to the idea. "It wouldn't be that big of a deal to switch the characters around and put Mario in a cage."

The more women who believed in themselves and their own strength, the better. Portia could be a princess who liked ball gowns, afternoon tea with the queen and being rescued by her Prince Charming all she wanted.

Juliet didn't like any of that. And didn't that put a knot the size of the crown jewels in her stomach?

Juliet might not like being rescued by the prince, but he'd had to do it just the same. Did he look down on her for not doing what she set out to do? Of course, if she hadn't been coming down with a stupid cold, the swim to Saint Tropez would have been within reach. That was her story and she was sticking to it.

He grinned and put his controller down, settling back against the couch, looking as if he'd humor her until next week if need be. "I'm sure Nintendo would love to hear your thoughts on how to stop perpetuating the stereotype of princesses always needing to be rescued."

"*You're* not even taking me seriously. Let alone a Japanese conglomerate that probably doesn't have one single female executive."

He tucked a lock of hair behind her ear, and she couldn't quite suppress the shiver his touch evoked. She didn't want to. Her stomach clenched. In anticipation *and* fear. Finn's blend of sexiness, solidness and tenderness scared her. Excited her. How messed up was that?

"I'm taking you seriously. I love how passionate you get about…well, everything. Your unwavering opinions define your character."

"You don't like it when I have an opinion. Especially not wh—" She bit down hard on her lip, so hard, the salty taste of blood seeped across her tongue.

Especially not when it's about how you should have acted a year ago.

"I love everything about you, Juliet," he said, and the catch in his voice thrummed through her chest. "I love that as strong as you are, you let me rescue you. I love that despite your seemingly inexhaustible determination, you're willing to ask me to help you take a bath. That's why we're a good team. We each play to the other's strengths and recognize our own limits."

Goodness. If she'd ever wondered why in the world she'd fallen in love with such a draconian, he'd blasted that curiosity to pieces. Where did he come up with such poetry?

"You don't have any limits," she grumbled to hide the thrill his heartfelt words had unfurled.

"That's not true. You almost pushed me past them in the bathtub earlier." The pad of his thumb caressed her jaw, and it was impossible to misinterpret the heat in his gaze.

It was just as impossible to ignore the answering liquid tug in her core. Despite everything, or maybe because of it, she longed to lose herself in the feelings he clearly still had for her and she for him. To lose her inhibitions and fears in his arms, his body, his drugging kisses, so mindless with pleasure, nothing else mattered.

Why did their relationship have to be so complicated? Why couldn't they be together, with all the difficulties of the outside world and their places in it forgotten? Nothing but the two of them, feeding their starving souls with each other. Just for a little while, with no one the wiser, no reminders of their impasse, no public eye to record every nuance of their interaction.

Her pulse beat in her throat.

Wasn't that what was going on *right now?* They were hidden away, held captive on this island, with no hope of rescue anytime soon. She could conceivably be off her stride for several days. Why not take advantage of their time together to enjoy the good parts of their relationship?

No one said they had to kiss *and* make up. Maybe they could just kiss…among other activities. King Laurent didn't dictate the rules. She could be with Finn whether his father liked it or not.

With no future to concern themselves with, no family to disappoint, she didn't have to worry about trusting him. If she kept her heart tucked away, he couldn't break it again. *No emotions. Ruthless determination.*

All they had to do was stay away from the past and focus on now. Piece of cake.

Eight

Later that day, Finn took a short break from monitoring Juliet's condition—or hovering as she liked to call it—and took a cold shower. It went a long way toward easing the ache that had taken up residence in his lower half. But not nearly long enough. He suspected only a naked and willing Juliet could completely eliminate it. That or a coma.

When he emerged from his bedroom, Juliet wasn't ensconced on the couch watching a chick flick where he'd left her. Clanking from the kitchen piqued his curiosity and he wandered into the melee of Juliet attempting to wrangle a pan and some meat into submission.

He watched her struggle for a minute, thoroughly enjoying the backside view of Juliet's slender, barefoot form. Except she was still sick and now he was all hot and bothered again.

"Why aren't you resting?" he finally asked.

The pan clattered to the Italian marble, cracking one

square tile in half. Ouch. Portia was going to have the king's head.

She whirled. "Don't sneak up on me like that."

"Sorry." He stomped in place a few times, mimicking just having arrived. "I'm in the kitchen now. Okay?"

"Okay." She grinned and turned to her stove-top project. "I'm not resting because you asked me to make you dinner."

"I did?" Had he hit his head? Obviously so, if he'd deliberately asked for a repeat of the Chicken With No Taste.

"Earlier. When you said I could show my gratitude by making you dinner." Gingerly, she nodded toward the back of the house and winced.

Ah, yes, on the bed, when he'd been holding on to his sanity by the tips of his fingers. That would definitely explain why he'd done something so unwise as to ask Juliet to make him dinner. "You're nowhere near well enough to be off the couch. Come on."

Sliding his hand into hers, he tugged her toward the living room, ignoring the blistering awareness of skin on skin.

"But you need to eat," she protested and dragged him to a halt between the two rooms.

"I've been feeding myself for twelve years." They were still holding hands but she didn't seem to notice. Far be it from him to bring it to her attention. He liked the feel of her delicate fingers against his. "I'll manage. What about you? Are you hungry? I can heat up some soup."

"Not really, thanks. I ate some crackers. Did I leave the stove on?" Peering over his shoulder, she sank teeth into the plump curve of her bottom lip.

His mouth tingled. That sweet swell of flesh was delicious, as he well knew from personal experience, and he couldn't tear his gaze away from it. "If you did, I'll take care of it."

She made a face. "I'm sure you will. Is there anything you can't take care of?"

Oh, he could think of one thing. A cold shower hadn't

helped his raging hormones catch a clue that first of all, Juliet wasn't in reconciliation mode, and second...

She sighed, pushing her breasts out invitingly. Before he lost his mind, he backed up, inadvertently stretching their locked hands.

She glanced down and tightened her grip, then closed the gap between them. "Wait, don't go. If you won't let me cook dinner, sit with me on the deck and watch the sunset."

Pure desire quickened through his gut.

"I...you probably don't need to be outside." Watch the sunset? Like, together? It almost sounded as if she wanted to spend time with him, in what she probably hadn't even considered would be a romantic setting—a complication he did not need. "You're still sick."

Did he sound as much like a song stuck on repeat to her as he did to himself?

"I don't feel that bad," she muttered, but her face was rosy in all the wrong places and her head tilted listlessly.

Cursing, he picked her up and deposited her on the couch before she could voice another objection. "At least sit down before you fall down. If you're bound and determined to show me your gratitude, get better. That's an order."

"Yes, sir." Flipping him a smart-aleck salute, she burrowed into the cushions and flung the blanket over her body, shoulders to feet. "Happy?"

Not in the slightest. Every nerve in his body ached with unfulfilled need. "Thrilled. We have plenty of time to watch sunsets after you get better."

She blinked up from her nest of blankets, innocent and alluring at the same time. He longed to crawl in with her.

"Sit with me then." She patted the couch and shot him a small smile he couldn't refuse.

In desperate need of a distraction, he sank onto the cushion and hit the power button on the TV remote. A Formula 1 race in Singapore, one of his top five favorite circuits, filled the screen. Automatically, he flexed his thumb to change the channel, but Juliet's hand covered his.

"This is fine," she said, and removed the remote from his suddenly nerveless fingers. "I'd like to watch this with you."

The roar of engines and whine of tires reverberated around them as he glanced at her askance. "I'd ask if you're feeling all right, but I already know the answer to that. Your fever must be worse than I thought if you're willing to watch a Formula 1 race."

"I told you I don't feel that bad. Tell me something. I've always wondered how you know which car is in first when they're going around the same loop over and over." Her temple came to rest on his shoulder as she squinted at the screen.

"The standings are listed in the ribbon across the top." More information about how to gauge the driver's position instantly sprang to his lips, but he bit it back. Surely she didn't actually care.

"Oh. That's easier than I thought it would be. How come some of the cars are identical and some are different?"

"The participants are on teams." Interest in the race completely lost, he tilted his nose toward her hair, inhaling the fresh scent of Juliet and the shampoo he'd used to wash her hair. The memory of her wet and naked under all those bubbles kicked up a slow torture.

She glanced up, puzzled, but clearly engaged.

"The teams have more than one guy driving," he clarified. "Same car, same team."

And for the next fifteen minutes, she asked more questions, patiently listening to his answers and occasionally offering an insightful comment about the ins and outs of the process.

"Planning to apply for a job as a pit crew member?" he asked after her questions tapered off. "You know, instead of teaching? Monaco has a track. You could jet over and back in thirty minutes tops."

She laughed. "Not a chance. I'd be too afraid to touch a million-dollar car."

"Then why all the questions?" An old thorn worked its way loose and poked him. Sporting events bored her and she'd never hidden her contempt for his interests. As she'd never hidden her contempt for his job.

"It's something you like. I wanted to learn more about it." Shrugging, she laced fingers with his casually, as she'd done a hundred times before they split up.

It felt different. Coupled with her nonchalantly tossed-out words, the effect was potent.

Her eyelids drifted halfway closed and she peeked up from under them. "So, what if instead of dinner, I wanted to show my gratitude some other way?"

The question came coupled with Juliet's lazy index finger trailing over his pectoral muscle and left no possibility of misinterpreting "some other way."

What was she doing? First Formula 1 and now this. The fever must be curdling her brain. And the fingertip hold on his sanity was sliding away at an alarming rate.

"You have a fever," he reminded her needlessly since they'd already discussed it at least five times. Or was the reminder more for his well-stirred blood's benefit? "I shouldn't even be this close to you."

"I seem to recall you've kissed me in the last twenty-four hours. More than once and quite thoroughly." She watched avidly for his reaction and he struggled not to give her one.

But he was pretty sure the instant hardening below the belt hadn't escaped her notice. No fabric in existence could disguise it.

"Face it," she murmured and the space between them, what little there was of it, vanished as she threw off the blanket, snuggling up against his chest. "You're already contaminated with my cooties. What's one more little kiss? To show my gratitude."

His gaze snapped to the firm, rosy lips so close to his. "You said we were over. On the beach. Is your near-death experience hindering your decision-making abilities?"

It was certainly messing with his.

This wasn't the plan. Rescue first. Reconciliation later. Too much unsaid lay underneath the surface to go down this path now. How could he even approach the subject of telling Juliet she was his father's choice for Finn's bride? He needed a cooler head, among other things, for that conversation.

She smiled and cupped a hand along his jaw. "Clarifying. Not hindering."

"Clarifying it how?"

How he put actual syllables together to form cohesive words, he'd never know. But *something* had shifted after she almost drowned, and despite protests to the contrary, he suspected it had affected her in a way he didn't fully trust.

"I'm still a prince and y—"

"Shh." Her thumb skated across his lips, silencing him. "Prince Alain isn't here. I only see Finn."

Finn. Yes, here on Île de Etienne, he could forget the complexities of that dual-edged sword and be nothing but a man. That yearning constantly simmered below the surface, and it thundered to life. They could get back to reality after they were rescued. Right now, he could indulge.

Involuntarily, his hands sought her face, determined to touch, desperate to connect. Cool skin met his palms. *Finally.* "I think your fever's gone."

"Is this the part where I get to say I told you so?" She grinned and nuzzled his throat.

"Sure. I can take it."

"Can you take this?"

Drawing him closer, until their breaths mingled, she brushed his lips with hers. Just a whisper of sweet contact, and instantly his mind drained of everything but the sexy, gorgeous woman in his arms.

"Yeah," he murmured against her mouth. "I can take all you've got of that."

Threading his fingers through her hair, he dived into the kiss with every intention of burning off the raging need for Juliet. They could deal with all the implications later.

She moaned and leaned into him as if she couldn't get close enough, her bewitching fingertips sparking across his neck and gliding under his T-shirt to spread at the span of his waist.

Yes, there. And everywhere else. He wanted her hands on him, wanted to touch her in kind, then slake his thirst for the woman he'd missed so very much.

His palms rested lightly against her throat as he angled her head to take her deeper into the kiss. She felt amazing.

The essence of Juliet poured into his senses. She slung a knee across his lap and climbed aboard, breasts teasing his chest, still slaying him with her mouth. Tongues slicked together, twining and seeking. Pleasuring.

He couldn't wait to sink into her tight, wet heat and let all his passion for Juliet explo—

With considerable effort, he twisted his mouth from hers. "We have to slow down, sweetheart."

Slow down.

Two words he'd never uttered in Juliet's presence. He had a bad habit of losing all common sense when she was within touching distance, and that needed to change *tout de suite.*

She lifted her head slightly and wiggled deeper into his lap. "Slow down? Why?"

Her confusion mingled with his frustration, adding weight to the already impossible situation his father had created.

"Because…" Struggling to simply breathe around the sharp desire clogging his system, he raked a hand through his hair before it found its way back into place on her very tempting rear.

Why? *Advantageous marriage. History. Scandal.* All of the above.

And for what was both the best and very worst reason of all. He could never be Just Finn, not even for a few moments, and it had been foolish to pretend he could.

"There's not one single condom in this whole house."

Juliet froze, hands on Finn's chest, as the significance sank in and her mind wheeled off in a dozen directions. "No condoms?"

So much for her plan to seduce Finn out of his clothes and indulge in a short-lived, no-hearts-required reunion. And here she thought the past and future were the complications they should avoid. Now he'd dragged the present into the equation.

"Not one. I've looked. Are you on some form of birth control?" he asked hopefully.

"No. Why would I be on birth control?" She'd spent the past year pretending she had no sex drive.

"Because you'd gone to a matchmaker to find a husband." He shrugged. "It was worth a shot to ask."

In actuality, she'd gone to a matchmaker because she was running away. Intimacy hadn't been forefront in her mind. Thank goodness Elise had saved one of her clients from being matched with Juliet—it would have been patently unfair to some poor man who could never compare with the man sitting next to her.

"So that's it? We can't do *anything*?"

She accompanied the question with a slow finger-walk down Finn's torso and kept going. He sucked in a breath as her nails grazed his still-impressive erection.

"If I'd known those fake nails would feel like that, I'd have bought you some a long time ago." He lifted her hand from his lap and held it against his thundering heart. "So you have to slow down."

"We can be careful." She tilted her hips back and forth, rubbing shamelessly against his rigid length. Heat shafted through her core and she arched involuntarily, grazing his chest with her sensitive nipples.

Thighs quivering, he groaned and thrust upward to meet her hip rolls. "There's no such thing as being careful when I've got you naked, especially if you keep doing that. I've spent the last year at the mercy of tabloids. A surprise pregnancy would be icing on the cake."

A baby. *Finn's* baby.

Sheer longing twisted through her insides, intense and shocking. Where had that come from?

"Sorry, I'll stop." She started to shift but his iron grip held her in place.

"I said slow down, not stop." His sizzling blue eyes sought hers and held them as he slowly circled his hips, grinding his erection against her.

"So," she gasped as the friction lit her up. "If you make love to me really slowly, that's going to prevent conception?"

Slow wasn't going to be an option much longer. She wanted every stitch of clothing between them gone. *Now.*

The wolfish grin on his face shot her arousal up another notch. "I'm more concerned about the out-of-wedlock part, not the pregnancy part."

She shook her head but the ringing in her ears got worse, not better. "What are you saying? That if we were married, it wouldn't be an issue?"

"If you get pregnant, we'd have to get married." His hands slid up both sides of her torso, thumbs hovering near her breasts, almost but not quite circling the aching peaks. "It's non-negotiable."

Her brain couldn't keep up, especially not with Finn's really good parts flush against hers and her nipples strain-

ing toward his thumbs, begging to be touched. "Is this a…
marriage proposal?"

Marriage. Finn was talking about *marriage.* To her.
While mere molecules of damp fabric separated her sex
from his.

"Not precisely." He pursed his beautifully chiseled lips,
and she couldn't tear her gaze from them. "More like a
promise of one to come."

A litany of jumbled emotions swirled through her head.
Her heart. She wanted him to love her. In the physical
sense. In the emotional sense. She flat-out wanted *him* and
her body didn't seem to care how she got him.

This was a really bad moment to realize she'd done a
poor job of tucking away all her feelings. Why had she
thought she could?

"Why can't we talk about this later?" she murmured and
leaned into his thumbs until they brushed her taut nipples.
Pleasure fluttered her eyelids and flooded her senses. "I
just want to be with you. Without all the complications. Is
that even possible?"

"Not between us, no."

She almost laughed at the irony. "Because you're Prince
Alain. Always."

His gaze sought hers, hot with desire and a significant
glint. "Because I'm still in love with you. It messes up everything. If only there was a way to forget about capital *H*
history and live right here in this moment, I'd do it, come
what may."

She blinked away sudden tears as his confession bled
through her body, singing through her pleasure center,
heightening everything.

Finn still loved her.

Her heart threw its doors open wide, sucking in the sentiment with glee. Something sweet and wonderful coursed
through her.

The concept of an island fling had been a poorly contrived pretext to feel exactly like that—without having to do the hard work of reconciliation. Without having to compromise or deal with her own guilt or risk allowing him to hurt her all over again.

"I shouldn't have said that." He shook his head. "I—"

"It's okay," she whispered, shocked her throat had spit out that instead of the *I still love you too* fighting to work free.

With effort so difficult it drew sweat, she slammed the door on her feelings. She couldn't tell him she loved him. That was how she'd given him the power to hurt her before, by making herself vulnerable.

But this time, she didn't have to.

He'd offered the perfect solution. They didn't have to rehash History or even mention it at all. They could be in the moment, indulge in the pleasure of each other and sort out the future later. Much later—especially the part about their feelings.

Slowly, she lifted the hem of her shirt, watching as his expression darkened.

"Let's forget about what happened a year ago and just be together. If there are consequences, so be it. Right here, right now, be Finn with me, even if you can only do it for one night."

Nine

One night.

Finn watched Juliet reveal her bra-less breasts, pulse beating in his temple in an erratic pattern more closely resembling Morse code than a rhythm designed to keep him alive.

Too much coffee. Too much Juliet. Too much at stake.

The sharp awareness and desire coursing through her expression quickened his blood, drawing his own desire to a fine point. Her breasts were breathtaking, gorgeous, rosy-tipped, and he wanted to run his tongue over the peaks until she cried out.

"Are you sure?" he asked her, his voice thready with anticipation.

If she chose to be with him, it wouldn't matter that the king had thrown them together. It wouldn't matter if she got pregnant as long as she understood marriage would be the next step.

"I'm sure," she said immediately. Decisively. It was heady to know she wanted him that badly.

But she was female and he'd made a cardinal error. "You're not letting the fact that I said I love you cloud this decision, are you?"

The feelings had sort of spilled out in reaction to the moment, without any forethought.

I love you was there in his consciousness, ready to be voiced as if he'd said it to her the day before. He didn't question whether she still loved him too—it was in her touch, in her kiss. In her eyes.

As was the total conflict she felt over it.

Which was why he didn't press her about her feelings. Why the choice had to be hers. This would be a real reconciliation, not one fabricated to serve the king's mandate, or it wouldn't happen at all.

But he was very close to losing control.

"No." A smile played at the corners of her mouth, as if she couldn't quite decide whether to let it flash. "This is about me and you and what we want. Grab hold and don't let go."

He knew exactly what he wanted. Tonight, he wanted to simply be Finn, to experience that harbor Juliet had always offered, where it didn't matter if he was merely the spare heir.

"Can you really forget?" he asked.

She held up a finger. "There's no past. No tomorrow. Just you and me and tonight. That's the only rule."

That sounded like a fine rule. If there was no tomorrow, his father's plan wasn't a factor. Besides, her family would never side with the crown, regardless of what happened between them, so the whole point was moot.

Without missing a beat, she leaned forward and placed her lips on his in a searching, questioning kiss. The heavens opened and poured light into his weakened soul.

Or perhaps that was Juliet's strength infusing his.

He slung his arms around her and clung to the woman he loved, imprinting the moment on his memory, so he could take it out later and savor it. She was the only woman he'd ever held who felt substantial enough to withstand the pressures and difficulties of being with a prince. She'd never crumble.

Unable to hold back a moment longer, he firmed his mouth and kissed her with every ounce of pent-up passion.

She moaned and opened under his onslaught. Eager to taste, he twined their tongues. Eager to touch, he pushed her torso forward, pressing her magnificent breasts to his chest.

"Need this gone," she mumbled and lifted his shirt over his head. As soon as she dropped it to the floor, her hands were back in place at his waist, fumbling with the closure of his pants and nearly ripping them off in her haste.

Yes. Naked. Now.

He lifted her to her feet and slid his pants off and then watched as she did the same with hers. He drew her against his body, peaks and valleys settling into familiar grooves, and finally they were bare flesh to bare flesh. Groaning with the sheer pleasure of her skin heating his, he took her mouth again in a savage kiss, teeth clacking and tongues thrusting.

There was no more need to slow down. And he didn't intend to.

Backing her up against the wall, he slid a thigh between her legs and rubbed her core, up and down, thrilling at the slickness that meant she was hot and ready for him. He knew her body as he knew his own. Knew how to touch her, how hard she liked it, when to let up and when to take her higher.

It was familiar, but that made it only more exciting. No guesswork, no confusion.

"Hurry," she moaned, heightening his own sense of urgency. "It's been so long. I want to feel you."

And he wanted to give her that.

Boosting her up, spine to the wall, he spread her thighs wide and teased her with the tip of his length. Her heat sizzled against his flesh and his eyes slammed shut at the shaft of pure lust spiking through his gut. He couldn't stand it. He eased her hips downward and sheathed himself one maddening centimeter at a time, desperately trying to give her as much pleasure as possible before he exploded.

With no barrier in place, sensation swamped him, rolling over his skin in a heavy tsunami of pleasure and spreading with wicked, thick heat.

Her amazing legs wrapped tighter around his waist, heels digging into his butt, urging him on with matched fervor.

"Unbelievable," she whispered. "You feel unbelievable."

"Tell me about it."

She rolled her hips, driving him deeper, and his knees buckled with the strain of holding back.

"Juliet," he murmured mindlessly and gurgled some more nonsense, unable to hold it all in.

She grabbed his free hand and put it against her nub, lacing her fingers with his to guide him. *Yes,* he loved it when she took charge. When she took her own pleasure. It was powerful, beautiful. Passionate. And it drove him wild.

As he rubbed, she arched, flinging her head back and crying out. She came with powerful shocks that squeezed him so exquisitely, his own release followed.

Sinking to the floor, he gathered her up and held her, slick torsos heaving in tandem. He smoothed her hair back from her forehead and just breathed, his mind, body and soul in perfect peace.

That was what he'd missed the most.

"Maybe next time we'll make it to the couch," she muttered and heaved a contented sigh that he felt clear to his knees. Her head thunked forward to land on his shoulder.

"Maybe next time you'll give me a chance to get near the

couch." Hence his point about the impossibility of "being careful." As if he'd have the capacity to pull out early once Juliet invited him into her slick heat. He'd have a better shot at swallowing the entire Mediterranean.

His lips found her temple and rested in the hollow. For the first time in the history of their relationship, neither of them had anywhere to be. They could make love all day long if they wanted to.

And he wanted to.

Tomorrow, the lack of outside pressures might abruptly end, and what kind of fool passed up an all-you-can-eat buffet?

As long as they were naked, he'd be happy to find a few dozen ways to keep both their brains occupied. Then, the little circle of peace that was Île de Etienne would stay intact. The past didn't exist, and the future wasn't here yet.

Finn didn't have to think about either.

They made it to the bed. Barely.

Juliet flopped back against the pillow and moaned as Finn tongued his merry way up her thigh, leisurely, as if they had all the time in the world. They didn't. Their island paradise was short-lived and besides, she wanted him inside her *now*.

"How do you make that feel so good?" she murmured and then cried out as his lips nibbled her with exactly the right pressure to light her up.

The white-hot pleasure arched her back so fast, her spine cracked. But then he stopped right as a hot wave radiated from her center, the precursor to another amazing orgasm.

Before she could protest, he flipped her onto her stomach, sandwiched her against the mattress and drove in from behind. *Yes, perfect.* It wasn't just his favorite position. It was hers too.

Her eyelids fluttered in ecstasy as he angled her hips to take him deeper, his mouth on her shoulder, chafing her skin with his unshaven jaw. She rolled her shoulder, shoving it between his lips and he complied with her unspoken request, sucking with indelicate pressure.

He eased out and back in again, slowly. Way too slowly.

She locked her ankles together to increase the friction, the way they both liked it. Groaning, he increased the pace, as she needed, at exactly the tempo he knew would launch her into oblivion. She squeezed once and that was it. Stars burst behind her eyes, blinding her for a moment.

He groaned as he collapsed on her back, his climax pulsing inside her deliciously.

She'd lost count of the number of times he'd rendered her boneless. The first one, against the living room wall, had been a near out-of-body experience. The rest had been full-body experiences, a revel in the corporeal as only Finn could deliver.

She remembered that he was good. But reality far eclipsed the memory.

The man was incredible, tireless, physical. When he got excited, he wasn't gentle, but she liked it a little rough, especially because she'd evoked it in the first place. It made a girl feel sexy to have a man slightly out of control over her. Besides, she gave as good as she got, and that only boosted his passion. Which in turn, fed hers.

No wonder they'd been matched. They fit together, like the hearts on the necklace Elise had given her, entwined by passion.

Finally he rolled and they separated. Breathing heavily, he flung an arm over his head and shut his eyes, shamelessly splayed like a bad girl's fantasy across the bed, naked and gorgeous. She drank in the sight and just as shamelessly enjoyed every second of it.

His well-developed chest muscles flexed and relaxed as he breathed. He had a new line of hard, defined ripples across his lower stomach, the result of what must be a new workout routine. She heartily approved of the addition to the contours of his body.

At the same time, sadness crept into her bubble of bliss. He'd developed those muscles over the past year. While they'd been apart. He'd lived a whole year's worth of life that she knew nothing about because his stubborn refusal to open his mind had driven them apart.

Not going there, she reminded herself.

They'd agreed on one rule—forget the past—and already she was trying to break it.

"Let's go outside," she suggested, determined to slide back into a state of mindlessness.

One of Finn's eyes popped open to regard her warily. "It's dark. And I must be rusty at this if you want to go outside instead of staying naked in bed. With me."

She laughed. "I never said anything about getting dressed. One thing we have a distinct lack of is neighbors and paparazzi. It's June, with perfect weather. When else will we have such a unique set of circumstances?"

His brows lifted. "Sex under the stars. I like it."

He rolled from the bed and yanked the comforter along with him, waggling his brows over his shoulder as he dashed from the bedroom.

She followed him, and the view of his bare butt was nice indeed. She sighed. It would be so great if she could count on being able to see it whenever she wanted.

Whose bright idea was it again to be together without thinking about the future? Oh, yeah—*hers*.

She squared her shoulders and shut the sliding glass door to the deck behind her.

A sweeping panorama of stars blanketed the still night, breathtaking in its splendor. The quiet lap of water provided a melodic soundtrack. A bright moon hung in the sky to the west, lighting the way to Spain.

"Wow," she said. "I should get extra points for coming up with this idea."

Finn lay back on the comforter he'd spread on the deck and patted it in a nonverbal invitation to join him. "I was just thinking about all the ways I planned to thank you for it. It's amazing."

She scooted next to him and he curled her into his body, flesh on flesh. His arm lay heavy against her side, fingers stroking the curve of her waist, but it was oddly absent of any sizzle. It felt…comfortable, and tranquility stole over her.

It could be like this back home in Delamer. Surely it could. They were doing a fine job of ignoring the past. Why not keep it up? Maybe not forever, but for a little while at least, dipping back into their relationship slowly.

The stars shone, sending light to Earth that had left years and years ago, before she and Finn had split up. Before life had grown so complicated. If only there was a way to get back to that.

For a long time, she'd considered herself as star-crossed as her name implied. But did it have to be that way? If they loved each other, why couldn't that be enough?

Finn hadn't mentioned marriage or love again, but she knew it wasn't because he'd changed his mind. Finn was nothing if not constant, and she loved that about him. She never had to question whether he'd waffled on an issue or if he'd considered all the facts before forming an opinion. He meant what he said and said what he meant. It was an inexorable part of his character.

For the first time since Bernard died, it seemed like more of a positive than a negative. She'd never have to wonder if Finn would fall out of love with her one day. Never wonder if he'd cheat on her.

"What if I said you could call me?" she blurted out. "At home. After we get off this island."

They could try dinner again, have a civilized conversation and sit on their hands lest they rip each other's clothes off in the cab on the way back to his place, where they'd make love until dawn.

His mouth rested against her forehead, and she felt his lips turn up. "We're a little past that stage, don't you think? By the end of the month, we could be engaged."

An image of Finn on one knee, a diamond as bright as a star extended between his fingers, exploded in her head. Her lungs burned as she held her breath, hoping that would make the image go away.

He didn't want to marry her, but he would—out of duty.

Gee, *that* was romantic. How had this simple night together gotten so messed up? She didn't want Finn to propose to her because he felt obligated to. Neither did she want this idyll to be over.

She sat up and twisted to look at him. "What if I don't get pregnant? That's it? *Au revoir* and don't call me, I'll call you?"

"That's rich, Juliet." He squeezed the bridge of his nose. "You're the one who came on to me, which is like pouring wine down the throat of an alcoholic and daring him not to swallow."

She processed his backhanded compliment. If she'd decoded his analogy correctly, he couldn't resist her. That put a small smile on her face for some unknown reason.

"Should I apologize?"

Finn swore in French. "Is this really the conversation you want to have?"

"I don't know. Everything feels so backward and crazy."

He heaved a sigh that carried all the way into her stomach, rolling it over with its intensity. "Don't you think about being together? Long-term?"

"Yeah," she whispered. She'd be lying if she said no.

"Then let's make that happen—with or without a baby to force the issue. If that's what you want."

That's what I want.

Instantly, the idea took root and she accepted it as gospel truth. A deep, shuddery breath nearly wrenched a sob loose.

But she couldn't have it both ways. Either they'd split up again or they'd be together. He was right—there was no *call me and we'll see how it goes.* Their relationship was too deep for that. Always had been, always would be.

"You can't marry me. Speaking of coronaries, *both* our families would have one."

Her mother would probably have a breakdown right there on the floor. That's why Île de Etienne was so perfect—no one had to know she'd indulged in a little fling with Finn.

Besides, Juliet could never marry Finn, not with the fear she'd find herself capable of using him to her own end fresh on her mind.

She bit her lip. But if she did get pregnant, was she prepared to lie about whom the father was? That wasn't even remotely possible. Finn would never agree to stay silent about having fathered her child.

And honestly, he'd be a wonderful father. She didn't want to raise a child alone or deprive her kid of all the joys of having a nuclear family. Deprive Finn of being able to see his son or daughter every day.

Ice picks of pain stabbed at the backs of her eyes. All she'd sought was an uncomplicated island adventure with a mouthwatering specimen of manhood who made her blood sing. Was that too much to ask?

"That's not true," he countered. "They wouldn't bat an eye if you were carrying my baby. Besides, my father's opinion of you has softened."

"When did that happen?"

"When he saw the photo of us together. It was in the note. He realized there was still something between us."

"Of course." That picture must have captured some serious sizzle to elicit such a drastic ploy as kidnapping.

"That's why he dumped us here, so we couldn't hurt his image any further by being photographed together."

"That's not why. You never gave me a chance to explain. My father had us brought here so we could spend time together, away from everything. See if a relationship was still possible." Sagging a little, he stared at the stars and she caught a hint that something was very off.

"Why in the world would he do something like that?"

"It must have been obvious I didn't want an arranged marriage any longer. But he still wants me to settle down, though I never dreamed he'd…well, that's why I tried so hard to flag down rescue. Spelled out the HELP sign. I didn't want us to reconcile like this, playing right into his hands. I'm sorr—"

"Don't let your father have any more control in our relationship." None of this should be about accidental pregnancy, or Finn's interfering father, but about the future and what making love actually meant for their relationship. "Tonight is just about us. Tomorrow, we can deal with everything else. Including your father, the past and the future. Let it go for now."

She tried to do the same. She really did. But that blanket of peace wouldn't return, no matter what tricks she employed to clear her mind. Because she couldn't stop wondering what was going to make tomorrow different from the past year.

The fates couldn't have conspired to put her and Finn together only to cruelly rip them apart.

Maybe other women waited around for fate to step in, but other women didn't get so much as a first chance with a man like Finn. Juliet Villere didn't leave her future to the hands of fate. And she wasn't blowing her second chance.

Tomorrow, *she'd* be the difference. Somehow.

They had to work through their issues once and for all, create a level playing field and never bring up the past again. She wanted to have their relationship back, intact, exactly as it had been, where she could depend on Finn to put her first above everyone else in his life.

Then she'd know for sure he loved her, for real, for forever.

Ten

When Juliet woke in the morning, she'd hardly opened her eyes before Finn rolled her against his side, intent clear as day in the sizzle shooting from his deceptively sleepy gaze.

"Good morning," she murmured, and snuggled into his warm body for an enchanting moment of pure harmony that had nothing to do with sex. She'd missed the small things that made life so much sweeter—good-night kisses, falling asleep holding hands, waking up together.

A moment was all she got to enjoy it. He thoroughly compromised her in twenty minutes flat, and she had the whisker burn in eight very tender places to prove it. To be fair, she'd left behind a few souvenir teeth marks on him.

"Good morning," he finally responded when he'd caught his breath. Sated and clearly determined to be lazy this morning, he turned on the TV and slung an arm around her companionably as they settled in to watch nothing.

His dark hair was still sleep-and-finger tousled and his chest unashamedly bare, all hard muscle and delicious skin for her tasting pleasure. She could get used to waking up to *that.* She couldn't stop looking at his beautiful form long enough to even register what channel he landed on.

Until he sat up, eyes hard and riveted to the screen. She glanced at the TV. A cable news station flashed a picture of a sinister-looking warship with deadly weapons scattered across the deck.

Finn hit the volume button and the news anchor's deep baritone filled the bedroom.

"…gathering off the coast of Greece, within striking distance of the newly assembled army. World leaders are meeting in Geneva this afternoon to discuss a preemptive hit on the country's forces."

His body tense, Finn glanced at her and she did a double take at the harsh lines around his mouth.

Juliet's pulse slammed into her throat. "What is he talking about?"

"In other news…" The anchor went on to describe a peace rally in Athens protesting the aggression.

"Whatever it is, it's not good," Finn said grimly. "That warship is stationed in the Ionian Sea. I could practically throw a rock and hit it from here."

Her fingers flexed to grab the remote and throw it across the room in kind. Military aggression. Her least favorite hot button.

This was a watershed moment, where she could let the wounds of the past rule or forge a new future. This warship's presence in the Mediterranean was important to Finn, evident in the stiff set of his jaw and the severe tilt of his brows.

"Find another channel talking about it," Juliet suggested softly. "You need to know."

Nodding, he flipped through the channels until he found a news station describing how the government of Alhendra, a small but well-financed country sandwiched between Albania and Greece, had sent missiles into a civilian neighborhood in Preveza, a beautiful Greek coastal region. The casualties were high and world powers' thirst for retaliation was higher. It was an unprovoked act of antagonism that the United Nations couldn't ignore and didn't intend to.

She forced herself to listen alongside him, and when he slid his hand into hers, she stiffened her shaking fingers to keep him from knowing how deeply ingrained her body's response was to seeing warships on the news.

Bernard's death had been reported with similar shots of a ship at full cruising speed, cutting through the dark waters of the sea. Over and over, they'd played that clip, with a scripted spiel about the accident.

A noise of pure disgust growled from Finn's throat. "I can't believe this is happening and I'm stuck here. Delamer might be in jeopardy. Any coastal region could get caught in the crossfire. Our ships can be ready to deploy and stand with our allies immediately. At the very least, we should send someone to Geneva."

Stuck here. With her. He'd rather be back home, reveling in his armed-forces glory.

"Don't you think your father is already on top of it?" she asked with raised eyebrows. "This is his moment in the sun."

Finn's too. It was a golden opportunity to espouse the virtues of his father's military polices. To give her a big, fat I-told-you-so and laugh off her earlier argument that it was peacetime.

He shot her a withering glare. "Of course he's on top of it. But he needs help. He's probably got someone on the way to get me right now. I should be there."

She'd been wrong before. *This* was the watershed moment. She had to accept that his sense of honor would never allow him to side against his father, no matter what the man did. She had to find a way to live with the fact that Bernard's death would not be avenged through reform.

Or she had to not be with Finn.

Which wasn't going to be much of a choice if she was carrying his baby.

Bernard had died but Juliet was still alive, and her brother wouldn't want her to be miserable on principle. He'd loved Finn and would never begrudge Juliet trying to find a future with the prince. Her parents would learn to adjust—or they wouldn't—but her family wasn't the reason her relationship with Finn had fallen apart a year ago.

It was because there was no compromise.

"We should spend the day setting up more signals, just in case your father plans to leave us here a while longer." Her head dropped, suddenly too heavy to hold up. She'd expected the day to unfold with a naked romp in the shower and then another naked romp through a couple of other choice locales. The disappointment melded with the shock, cracking her voice. "If several countries are sending forces to the Ionian Sea, they have to pass right by here. Someone will surely see us this time."

Their island fling-slash-reconciliation-slash-precursor to a marriage proposal had screeched to a halt.

Gently, he tipped her head up to meet his gaze, and she blinked back the moisture she'd been trying to hide. He was watching her with dark intensity that unleashed a shiver.

"I love you," he murmured. "That's not going to change, no matter what happens."

Whether she'd conceived. Whether she hadn't. Whether their families intervened in their relationship or didn't. Whether the world stood at the brink of war or not.

"I know."

Because she loved him like that too. And it messed up everything because she still hated his fervor for the military. Hated that he might die like Bernard and abandon her again, but this time forever.

Recognizing there was no compromise wasn't the same as being okay with it. And she wasn't. She couldn't be. Could she?

Maybe this wasn't real love or else it wouldn't feel so much like one—or both—of them had to give up everything.

Or was this simply proof that love *wasn't* enough?

He shook his head. "No, I don't think you do. I don't think you could possibly understand how completely torn up I am at this moment."

Her laugh wasn't nearly as bitter as she'd have expected. "I have a pretty good idea."

"I know this is hard for you. I know what it cost you to bite back your opinion of my father and of my job. Don't give up your convictions. I don't ever want you to give up, especially not on something you truly believe in."

Her pulse hammered in her throat. He'd never said anything like that before. It almost sounded as if he admired her for taking a stance against his father.

Maybe she'd misjudged his reasons for not siding with her. As many times as they'd argued over the protest, they'd never really talked rationally. Shouted, accused, defended—yes. Well, mostly she did that. Diplomacy wasn't in her DNA.

Worse, when diplomacy wasn't one of her skill sets, how effective of a princess would she really be? If a marriage proposal could potentially be imminent, perhaps she should practice being diplomatic a whole heck of a lot more. What better place to start than with History?

If they could successfully navigate that, they could endure anything and still make it. She'd finally feel safe enough to confess she'd never fallen out of love with him.

Finn shoved food in his mouth, but he couldn't have said what it was for any price.

He kept waiting to hear the sound of rescue approaching. The whine of a boat engine. The drone of helicopter blades. The longer the silence stretched, the worse his muscles knotted with tension.

Surely the king wouldn't leave Finn here marooned on Île de Etienne while warships convened just across the Mediterranean. It was unthinkable.

At the same time, he'd rather keep the real world at bay and stay completely submersed in this new Juliet who watched Formula 1 and didn't slice him open with arguments against military force.

He glanced at her, and she was so gorgeous in a simple red sundress that set off fireworks in her brown hair. She smiled, and it yanked a long slice of warmth from his center. They were sitting at the table, eating breakfast like a normal couple.

Something had happened to get them here. Dare he hope it was enough?

Well, he obviously did dare because hope of the most dangerous kind had begun to live in the back of his mind. Dangerous because he wanted to sweep Juliet off her feet with an outrageously romantic marriage proposal—before she handed him a pregnancy test. Before he had to take up his uniform and rejoin the Delamer Navy in what might devolve into combat. Search and rescue was his day job, but he was still a lieutenant in the armed forces. And his country was worth defending, even with his dying breath.

Securing a "yes" from her before all that other stuff interfered would make everything else bearable. They'd be together, they'd be in love and nothing else could touch them.

But he couldn't propose as he envisioned because they'd done nothing to address capital *H* history, not that he was complaining. He'd rather they didn't talk about that at all, except if they got married, she'd have to understand the obligations that came with being his princess. No more protests.

And she hadn't actually told him she loved him yet.

The timing was wrong. He couldn't propose until all the issues were addressed. *All* of them.

Juliet lifted a lock of hair from her shoulder and twirled it absently as she contemplated him. "You gonna eat that or massacre it?"

He glanced at his hand, which was pulverizing what appeared to have once been a slice of bread. "Both."

Shoving it in his mouth, he chewed and swallowed the evidence, but he barely tasted it.

They *had* to talk. And he'd put it off too long already.

In addition to dealing with History, it was important that she find out about her family's renewed attacks against his father from Finn and not from whoever came to rescue them. The only way this reconciliation would work was if she understood he had no intention of using their relationship to influence her family. But if she loved him, she'd take care of it on his behalf.

"You're so tense, I could cut this butter with your clenched jaw alone," she commented mildly and nodded to his plate. "You done with that?"

"Yeah." If they were both finished eating, now would be the optimal time to get started on that long-overdue discussion. The sooner, the better.

"Good."

Standing so abruptly her chair crashed to the floor, she slid the plate to the other side of the table and nestled into his lap, front to front, fitting into the planes of his body. Instantly, he hardened against her soft core, which radiated heat through her panties.

Or they could talk later. Much later.

Relieved to descend into that place where they connected brilliantly, he snaked a hand under the bright swatch of skirt and palmed her backside, teasing her with light fingertip trails. Then he delved beneath the silky fabric to trace her feminine contours.

Her breath came faster, and desire bloomed across her expression. It thoroughly thrilled him. Hips thrusting and circling, she threw her head back and rode hard against his rigid length. Desperate to get to flesh, he thumbed beneath the scrap of cloth covering her and fused his lips to her throat as he plunged two fingers into her wet heat.

Hot, so hot. Her, the position, his skin.

He wanted to feel her on the inside, let his mind drain of everything but the sensation of loving her.

His spine tingled from holding back his own release. She rocked on his hand faster, then faster still, moaning her pleasure, arching back against the table and spreading her thighs wider.

"That's it," he murmured as her eyelids slammed shut in ecstasy and her core throbbed against his fingers. She came on a cry that shafted through his groin, both painful and erotic at the same time.

She collapsed against his chest and he caught her, binding her close. Her head landed on his shoulder, grinding her core against his inflamed erection.

She made him *insane.*

"Strip," she commanded in his ear without shifting her weight. Or offering to help. Or shedding her dress.

"Easy for you to say." But he lifted her one-handed and wiggled out of his clothes. Gracelessly, for sure, but who cared?

Since she appeared to have lost the ability to work a single muscle group, he hiked up her dress, yanked the panties aside and lowered her onto his shaft. The spiral of heat and light exploded in a whirlwind, sucking him into the oblivion of her body.

Finally, she came alive. Rolling her hips, she took him higher, deeper, faster, and the dual edges of the corporeal and the emotional crashed, culminating in a release of epic proportions that could be fully expressed only with the "*I love you*" that spilled from his mouth, rained from his consciousness, radiated from his soul.

At least he thought he said it out loud. But she didn't say it back.

He willed away the prickliness at the back of his neck. They were just words. Saying them or not saying them didn't make the fact any less true. She loved him. He knew that.

When he found the energy, he stood, easily picking her up along with the motion, and carried her to the bed they'd shared last night. There, he drove them both into the stratosphere again, but it was slightly bittersweet this time. He refused to examine why.

Later, as they lay draped across the mattress, he stroked her hair. "Hey, I'm not so tense anymore."

She turned her head to face him and rested a cheek on the sheets, a grin stretching her lips. "Mission accomplished."

Some perverse tendency compelled him to rock the boat. "You know this is all about to end, right?"

A wrinkle appeared between her brows. "Which part?"

"The island-seclusion part."

"Oh. Yeah, we were supposed to be setting up flares or something, weren't we?" She drew his palm to her lips and mouthed a wet kiss along the crease. "You distracted me."

"Ha. It was the other way around. I was about to bring up another topic entirely."

"We have to talk. I know." She sat up, taking his hand with her and clutching it to her heart. "I think I'm ready."

"You look like you're about to march up the steps to the guillotine."

"We've been putting this off for a reason. It's painful. And it sucks," she whispered. "We haven't dealt with Bernard. Or the protest. And we have to if we're going to be together. I just don't want to. I'm not very good at expressing myself without yelling."

The tension was back, tenfold, cramping his well-used muscles. "What is there to yell about? We agreed to forget about history and move forward."

Obviously that wasn't going to work, not that he'd really believed it would.

"Forget about it for how long? Until they bring you home in a body bag?" She dragged a pillow over her face, but it didn't muffle the heart-wrenching sob as much as she probably hoped.

"Hey." He ran a thumb over her one uncovered shoulder. "That's not yelling. I was promised yelling. Toss that pillow off and let me have it."

Actually, he liked it better when she yelled. That, he understood. They argued, they yelled, they made up. Except for that last epic fight a year ago...

Her laugh eased his tight gut more than he'd expected. They were going to get through this. They were stronger this time. Wiser. More determined.

She peeked out from beneath the pillow. "Rain check? I'd like to look back on this conversation and call it rational. I guess hiding doesn't exactly scream nice and sane." She heaved a sigh and flipped the pillow toward the headboard. "I grew up invisible. Too many kids in the house, I guess. You were the first person who saw *me*. Who loved me for who I was, not what I could do for you. When Bernard died...you refused to listen to me, refused to see I might have valid ideas about changes. It hurt. I felt abandoned and lost. I don't know how to get over that."

She'd told him variations of this before, but never with such brokenness. Never without shouting it, along with as many inventive slurs on his intelligence as she could come up with. He definitely liked the shouting better. It gave him permission to shout back and never deal with the emotions being stirred up.

With that sucker punch ringing in his ears, she twisted the dual-edged sword. "When I see warships on TV, it brings it all back. I want to be with you. But I need you to choose me as well or I can't."

Rational. It was a good goal. And suddenly he wasn't so sure he could comply with it.

"What does that look like, Juliet? How can I help you feel like I'm choosing you?" he said, picking his words carefully lest he lead the witness toward a conclusion neither of them could live with.

"I need to feel like you honor our relationship above all others. Like you're on my side. Especially when it's about an issue that destroyed my family."

There it was. He couldn't pretend to misunderstand. Not this time. But if she could do this without yelling, he could too.

Because he loved her and she was trying to do things differently.

He jackknifed to his knees and took her face between his palms. "I want you to understand something critically important. If I was a regular guy, Finn the helicopter pilot who digs this girl Juliet from down the road, I'd crawl over broken glass for a hundred miles to make you mine forever."

Something equal parts tender and shattered flashed in her eyes, gutting him instantly. Because she knew he wasn't finished.

And he wasn't. He couldn't bow to her demands just because she preferred it.

"But I'm not that guy. I don't want to be that guy because being Prince Alain Phineas of Montagne, Duke of Marechal, House of Couronne is a privilege. One I'm honored to live up to."

"So what are you saying?" she whispered, her gaze darting over his face. "*Au revoir* and don't call me, I'll call you?"

"No." He dropped his hands to his side. "That means I'm standing on the other side of a huge expanse of middle ground. I need you to meet me in the middle if we're going to work outside of Île de Etienne."

There. He'd said it as plainly as he could.

"Compromise." She nodded once. "If that's what it takes, that's something I can work with."

Relief jump-started his pulse. "Then you finally understand. You see how important the military is to me. It's part of me. Part of my identity."

Confusion marred her expression and she crossed her arms. "I thought your title was your identity. That you were honoring your blood. I don't see how the military is suddenly rearing its ugly head into this conversation. One has nothing to do with the other."

So she *didn't* get it. "They have everything to do with each other. Alexander's role is clearly defined. He's going to be king. What am I going to be? Prince Alain, the same thing I am now and always was. There's nothing special about me. Nothing I can do to make a contribution except provide defense for the country my father leads."

That, and marry advantageously. The thought added a ninety-stone weight to his shoulders.

"Oh, my darling." Her lips trembled and she clamped them shut. "You're the most special man I've ever known. Alexander was born to his role, but it's so narrow. You have the opportunity to make yours whatever you want it to be. You can be known as the prince who makes a difference in the lives of his people. By introducing reform to the mandatory service law. Get your recruits the right way, from those who choose it, instead of making it a requirement."

"The military is mine, Juliet," he bit out. "Reform isn't on the table."

Why were they having this conversation again? To prove History always repeated itself?

"I see." Her gaze hardened. "You're all for compromise as long as it's me who's doing the compromising."

"I'm all for both of us showing our respect and affection by honoring the other's position." This was the critical point, the one she had to get through her head. "If you love me, you can't only love part of me. You have to love the whole me, including the part that doesn't agree with you."

"Same goes." She took a deep breath, her bare breasts rising and falling in sync. "Have you ever considered that I am honoring my blood too? Bernard was my brother, and his memory deserves nothing less than my strongest convictions. You said I should never give them up. Are you going back on that now?"

Of course he'd considered that. Finn had a brother too. "No, I meant it. Integrity is important to me. I wouldn't love you if you didn't have those convictions."

"Integrity is important to me too. The fact that you stand so strongly in yours is partly why I'm here having this discussion instead of storming out."

That made two of them. But storming out was sounding better and better the longer they beat their heads against this wall between them. If they couldn't resolve things here without any outside pressures, how could they do it at home?

That was the reason he didn't storm out. Once they left Île de Etienne, it would be too late. They had to break down that wall here and now.

"Family is as important as integrity," he said. "To both of us. Honoring the other's position includes helping our families understand it, as well. You realize if we're together, your family can't continue opposing my father, right?"

From outside the house, the distinctive, unmistakable *thwack, thwack, thwack* of helicopter blades split the air. Juliet whirled toward the sound as if she'd been thrown a lifeline.

No. Not yet.

But willing away rescue didn't work any better than willing it here had. He'd run out of time.

Eleven

The drone of a helicopter cut off the last of Finn's sentence, but Juliet had heard enough of it to be simultaneously sorry and thrilled the king had finally sent someone for them.

Part of her wanted to hop on the helicopter and pretend they'd dealt with all their issues. The rest of her knew that wasn't going to work.

Slowly, she faced Finn, tamping down her rising temper with considerable effort. "My family can't oppose your father or I can't?"

"Neither. I can't take any more scandals. Or protests."

"Or what? Your father won't allow us to be together? This isn't the Dark Ages."

How long did they have until whomever was sent to retrieve them reached the door? They weren't even dressed, something she was happy to take care of. She needed something to do with her hands.

"My father isn't—" Finn thumped the bed in apparent frustration. "This is about you and me and our future. If we're married, you'll be a princess of a country that requires eighteen-year-old males to serve three years in the armed forces."

She paused in the process of slipping on the red dress she'd worn for a grand total of thirty minutes thus far today and glanced at him over her shoulder. "Yeah. That doesn't mean I have to agree with it."

"No, you don't. But you can't freely declare your disagreement. That's the point."

"Fine, then don't marry me." Her chest ached at the pronouncement. "We can be together without getting married. Couples do it all the time, and it solves every problem in one shot, right? It'll even make your father happy."

"It wouldn't make me happy. Besides, this—" his hand cut a zigzag line in the air, indicating the house at large "—was a chance for us to rekindle our relationship, remember? My father wants us to get married."

"What?" The king *wanted* them to get married?

Scooting to the edge of the bed, he pulled on his clothes without looking at her. "I told you that's what this was about."

Something seemed off. She couldn't put her finger on it. "Not the marriage part. I would have remembered that."

"Because it was irrelevant." He yanked his shirt over his head and then raised his eyebrows. "One night. No past, no future. That was your rule. It's tomorrow and we're talking about it."

"Yeah, because yesterday, I thought all we had to work through was the past. Your father wants us married. What don't I know?"

He shut his eyes for a beat, which didn't settle the sudden swirl in her stomach. "Let's just say you're my advantageous marriage."

Like a behind-schedule bullet train, her pulse rocketed into the triple digits. Being dressed didn't provide nearly the shield she'd have expected. "Oh, no, let's *not* just say that. Let's say a whole lot more."

"Your family renewed their attacks against my father." Finn locked gazes with her, his expression dark. Too dark. "If we're a couple, their position is neutralized. It looks like you're siding with the crown."

Dizziness rushed up out of nowhere, knocking her off balance.

This was a setup to get her family to back off. A sharp pain tore through her chest and kept going. Nausea churned up her stomach, and she swallowed against the burn rocketing up the back of her throat.

A *setup.* "And you went along with it."

"I didn't." He fairly bristled with the denial. "I would never use our relationship to influence your family. But if we're married, you see the trouble with continuing to protest Delamer's laws. Don't you?"

That had been the goal all along—get that Villere family to shut up. And she'd fallen for it without a peep of protest. "I slept with you. I was *intimate* with you. Because I thought you wanted to be with me. But it was all a lie. How could you do that?"

"I gave you a choice." His hands flew up in protest, palms out as if he intended to mime his way out of trouble. "I slowed it down even though I absolutely wanted to be with you. For exactly this reason, so you would know you made that choice, not me."

If you get pregnant, we'd have to get married.

A cloud of red stole over her vision and the most unladylike word she knew slipped out, verbalizing her rising distress.

There were no condoms in this house *by design.*

And she'd walked smack into it. This wasn't just his father's plan. Finn had bought into it, made it his own, twisting it into something so brilliantly diabolical, it nearly doubled her over.

"I made that choice without all the facts!" she shouted over the *snap* of her heart breaking.

Oh, God, without *any* of the facts. She'd been so worried about making sure her own motives were pure, that she wasn't using him for her own gain. It never occurred to her that he might not have the same compunction.

He'd been using her. All along.

Unforgivable.

She'd been trying so hard to figure out how to live with his refusal to compromise. Because she'd truly believed that the deficiency was hers. That she couldn't possibly understand the royal pressures he faced and if she wanted to be with him, she'd have to give more than he did.

She'd allowed herself to be vulnerable. To lay out her hurts and fears, trusting that he'd keep her feelings safe.

That might be the worst part of all.

"You had the important facts." His gaze sought hers as if he had a prayer of communicating something nonverbally. "Like that I love you."

Ha. That wasn't a fact. That was the purest fiction.

"*This* is your definition of love? Lying to me and using me?"

He'd used her body, but far worse, he'd used her feelings against her. In the end, it hadn't mattered if she'd told him she loved him or not. He still managed to eviscerate her anyway.

Bang, bang, bang. The helicopter pilot was at the front door.

Finn's forehead wrinkled but it was the only outward indicator that her words had any effect. "I didn't lie to you. I never saw you as my advantageous marriage. Actually, I wasn't even sure we'd work things out, especially not this way. But everything snowballed and I wanted you to hear about your family's renewed fervor from me. I didn't want you to find out from…"

"Finn?" The male voice called out from the living room.

"Alexander," Finn finished.

Crown Prince Alexander of Montagne filled the doorway of the bedroom, larger than life, and a grimace on his face. "What happened to my patio furniture?"

"This is *your* house?" Juliet truly thought she'd lost the capacity to be shocked. But apparently the deception went much deeper than she'd ever guessed. Finn had known that from the beginning too. No wonder the house was stocked with games and food that Alexander and Portia liked.

Alexander, to his credit, didn't flinch at Juliet's version of a royal address. But she wasn't too thrilled with any member of the House of Couronne at this point in time, thank you very much. Royalty earned fealty in her humble opinion, and being a party to kidnapping one of his subjects hadn't endeared Prince Alexander to Juliet in the slightest.

Finn threw up a hand in his brother's direction. "Can you give us a minute, please?"

"Only a minute." Alexander crossed his arms, and it was easy to imagine him piercing the members of Parliament with that same regal glare. Which he could jolly well go off and do. There was no room for another insufferable prince in this horrific situation.

He backed away and disappeared.

"Juliet. For what it's worth, I'm sorry. I could have done this differently." Finn approached her and reached out as if to touch her and then changed his mind at the last minute. Smart man. But not smart enough.

She gathered great gobs of red skirt in both fists before she decked him. "Why didn't you do it differently then? Why didn't you tell me?"

"I—" He sighed. "I honestly didn't think you'd take it like this."

"What, like if I got pregnant, you'd marry me and use that to force every Villere in Delamer to keep quiet?"

His head bowed. "That wasn't the plan. The plan was to get off this island. Then when we got home, I was going to call you and see if we could start over. Things happened. You started coming on to m—"

"I'm going to get in that helicopter with Alexander because I have to." There was *no way* he was pinning this on her. "Once we hit Delamer, I'm going to get out and I never want to see you again."

"Don't say that." His eyes glistened with vulnerability she could hardly stomach. "This reconciliation was real. Don't let the admittedly unusual circumstances take away from that. We can make it work."

Her laugh shot out with surprising ease. "There was no reconciliation. We might have been headed toward one, but don't fool yourself. We still had a lot to work through, and this last bit erased any progress. You still can't see that you not only didn't take my side, you took your father's. There's nothing you can say or do in a million years that would make that okay, that would put us near the realm of 'making it work.' Nothing."

"There's still the possibility of pregnancy."

His trump card. The tips of her ears burned with the mere mention of the word *pregnancy.* That was probably the hardest part—that if she got pregnant, they wouldn't be rejoicing over it together, as she'd stupidly let herself envision.

"Maybe. But it won't involve a wedding or a happily-ever-after. Stay away from me. I mean it."

He'd never know either way. If she'd conceived, she'd never ask him for a single tiny diamond from the crown jewels to support her or the baby.

For the rest of her life, she'd have to see Finn's eyes in her baby's face. That was her punishment for trusting him again.

"You can't mean that. You have the keys to my heart." Finn slapped his chest in the spot where the organ in question was supposed to be—but wasn't—and his mouth softened. "It's not a throwaway cliché. You have the ability to unlock it from the outside and come in without my permission. Rifle around and romp through me intimately. Use that power wisely."

He meant she could hurt him. And she fully intended to ensure he hurt every bit as much as she did.

Finn watched Juliet out of the corner of his burning eyes as she huddled against the helicopter seat without speaking to either him or Alexander.

Fragile and broken, she wore her bruised emotions like a cloak. She hurt and it was his fault.

How had this turned out so badly? They couldn't even talk over the whack of the blades and the rush of air as they flew toward the shore. But what else could he say? She'd made her point quite clearly—she wanted him to choose her, and in her mind, he hadn't.

As soon as Alexander touched down east of the palace, she launched from the helicopter and scurried toward the gatekeeper without a backward glance.

"I'm assuming that didn't go well," Alexander said wryly.

"Shut up. The kidnapping was a stupid idea from the beginning." Finn debated whether to follow Juliet and throw himself at her feet or keep what little of his pride remained and let the gatekeeper call her a taxi.

He turned toward the house, slashing the remainder of his heart from his chest. There wasn't anything else he could do but let her go. She wasn't in love with him. She'd probably never really loved him. After all, someone who loved him wouldn't have participated in the protest in the first place. If she loved him, she would have said so at least once, especially after he said it to her.

Her interest in Formula 1 had probably even been by design—to butter him up so she could get what she wanted.

"I told Father that," Alexander said in his typical matter-of-fact and annoyingly brief fashion.

That answered the question of whether his brother had been in on the king's plan too. Of course Alexander had been the one sent to fetch them. The fewer people who knew about what the king had done, the better, no doubt.

Not many people could fly a helicopter anyway. Alexander had fallen in love with piloting helicopters during his three years of mandatory service but now had to do it on the sidelines. He couldn't fly in combat. But Finn could. And when Finn served his three, he'd vowed to do that one thing better than his brother.

Thus far, he had. It was his calling, his first love. And maybe he tended to be a little protective of it. A long wave unsettled his stomach. Juliet might have recognized that well before he had.

"Why didn't you come get me earlier then if you realized it wasn't going to work?" Finn's fist doubled and he longed to take out his frustration on someone who matched him in strength and skill, who could take whatever he dished out and then some. Someone other than Juliet.

Alexander clapped Finn on the shoulder as they mounted the steps to the palace. "I said it was stupid, not that it wouldn't work. I actually thought you'd pull it off."

And didn't that rub salt in the wound? Not only had he not succeeded, but Alexander's glib comment devalued the emotional aspect of what had happened. As if Finn had merely been trying to land a large account or net a sizable income from an investment. "It was doomed to failure from the start because Juliet is too stubborn."

"Must have been like looking in a mirror then."

"What's that supposed to mean? You think I'm stubborn?"

"As a fish on a line that refuses to come out of the water." Alexander tilted his head. "We don't call you Finn solely for your ability to swim, my brother."

Smirking to hide the bloody trails Alexander had carved

through him, Finn flipped back, "Thanks for the pep talk. It's been hugely helpful."

Even his brother was against him.

Finn ached to take his wounded soul to the kitchen, where the palace cook would look the other way if he stole some leftovers from the refrigerator and a cabernet from the wine cellar. The refuge of his childhood called to him, but he swallowed it away.

Prince Alain didn't have the luxury of hiding or licking his wounds.

"Is Father in residence?" Finn asked instead. "I need to be briefed on the situation with Alhendra."

The crown prince nodded and jerked his head. "In his study."

Finn hadn't lived at the palace in twelve years, but it still welcomed him every time. Footmen called, "Prince Alexander. Prince Alain," as they passed, heads inclined. Maids smiled and bobbed. Finn gave each one a return nod or smile and prayed they didn't take offense if it wasn't entirely heartfelt.

The king glanced up as his sons entered his study. "Excellent timing, Alexander. Finn, good to see you, son."

Respectfully, both men waited for their father to continue speaking in deference to his station.

King Laurent stood and leaned a hip on the desk, as was his habit when doling out difficult news. "Tension is high with our friends in Greece, Italy and Turkey. We're going to send all four of our warships, and it's not going to be well received by the whole of Delamer's population. I trust you have good news for us in that regard?"

Finn shook his head as his stomach rolled. Alexander had excellent timing but Finn's was horrific—now would have been the opportune time to be announcing his engagement to Juliet Villere.

Yeah. He could see how Juliet had taken everything the wrong way.

"Juliet did not find the idea of marrying me to her liking." Finn laced his hands behind his back and spread his legs to brace for the full brunt of the disappointment to come.

His father's mouth flattened into a thin line. Because Finn had failed on every level to deliver to the king's expectations.

"That's unfortunate."

A tiny, inadequate word to describe what it truly was. "Yes, sir."

The king's gaze sliced through Finn and he was seventeen again, being called on the carpet to explain why he hadn't danced with the King of Spain's daughter at a charity ball. Or why he hadn't scored as high on his mathematics baccalaureate as Alexander. Why by age twenty-seven, he hadn't been promoted to captain. The past year had been full of such carpet-treading moments, especially when the photo surfaced of him twined with a leggy blonde on a pool table.

"The relationship is unrecoverable then?" his father asked, his forefinger tapping thoughtfully on his chin, as if they were discussing the budget for the country's infrastructure instead of his son's unhappily-ever-after.

"Yes, I'm fairly certain it's over forever this time."

The cramp in his chest blindsided him and he blinked away moisture from the corners of his eyes. Hopefully no one had noticed him being such a girl.

How was he supposed to get through this? Juliet had a bad habit of breaking his heart and he had a bad habit of letting her. But this time, it wasn't solely her fault. Despite his comment to Alexander, Juliet's stubborn nature wasn't fully to blame.

The die had been cast when the photographer snapped that picture at Elise's party back in the States. Once his father put the kidnapping in motion, things couldn't have played out differently. If his father hadn't kidnapped them,

Juliet never would have spoken to him again anyway—of that, he was certain.

And even if she had, clearly they lacked whatever was needed to finally resolve their history. Worse, she'd never side with the crown. What new disaster might Finn have invited into his life if he'd returned from Île de Etienne engaged, only to have Juliet create another scandal?

"Well, then." The king paused, nodding. "We need to find another way for you to be useful."

Useful. It was the only thing Finn had ever wanted from his father—to be told he wasn't the spare heir but someone with value and importance. Just like Alexander. "I'm happy to do whatever's required of me."

"You're hereby ordered to report to the bridge of the *Aurélien.*" The king's eyebrows drew together over his uncompromising and authoritative gaze. "If you can't inspire a girl to marry you, maybe you can inspire a country to back down."

A second chance. Finn latched on to it with gratitude. He could still make a difference.

"I can." He would, gladly. It was a place to vent his frustration and aggression, spending it all on the backs of Delamer's enemies.

"I wish I could be there." The slight wistfulness in Alexander's tone didn't escape Finn.

"The front line is not your place," Finn said as gently as he could, suddenly glad he had the freedom to take a few more risks.

Alexander was born to his role, but it's so narrow. Juliet's voice floated to him on a wisp of memory. *You have the opportunity to make yours whatever you want it to be.*

Uneasily, he shifted from foot to foot. He'd spent the bulk of his life feeling inferior to the crown prince. Perhaps he'd viewed his birth order with too limited a lens.

Had Juliet broadened his vision that much in a few short

days? They'd dated for nearly a year the first time without any such revelations. Seclusion had positives, too.

Instantly, he was back on Île de Etienne, lying with Juliet on a blanket with the heavens opened above them and talking about making it work long-term. He missed her so much, it weakened his knees for a moment.

"Yes, your brother is needed at home." The king's odd half smile had Finn doing a double take.

"Portia's pregnant," Alexander explained.

The word hit Finn square in the solar plexus. Pure jealousy warred with the joy his brother's announcement evoked. He was going to be an uncle.

But in that moment he wanted to be the one announcing his impending fatherhood, the one with that glint of pure awe and amazement shining from his eyes. At this very moment, Juliet might be pregnant—and Finn had ruined any chance of having a relationship with the mother of his child. Would she even tell him if she'd conceived?

"Congratulations," he choked out.

"Thanks. She's having…complications. It's been a little touch and go. The doctor has her on one hundred percent bed rest and there's still a possibility she could lose the baby." Concern for his wife added a weight to Alexander's voice that Finn didn't recall hearing before.

It never occurred to him that his brother might be walking such a difficult path while Finn had been off frolicking in Alexander's house and drinking his wine.

"Well, of course you can't ship out with the rest of us. Take care of Portia and your child. That's the most important thing you can be doing," Finn said firmly. "I'll take up the mantle of defense."

If that defense required him to lay down his life for his people, he would do that without a whimper. Juliet was one of them after all, and now, he had a whole lot more to defend. Portia was carrying the heir to the Delamer throne.

Finn's only regret was that he would go out with his relationship with Juliet so fractured.

Twelve

Home. Juliet threw her arms around her mom, and the smell of fresh bread and cinnamon in her mother's hair was enough to finally thaw Juliet's flash-frozen internal organs, which had seized up during the interminable helicopter ride with the Royal Duo.

"We've been worried." Her mom smoothed Juliet's hair, as she used to when Juliet was little. "We called your cell phone so many times without an answer. We finally tracked down Elise Arundel and she said you'd gone on an extended vacation with the prince. We were not expecting him to be your match."

Elise. The king must have contacted her and made up some story about Juliet and Finn jetting off to an exotic locale to reconnect, conveniently leaving out the part where they hadn't done so under their own volition.

At least Elise hadn't been left to worry. The king got a tiny minutia of a point for that.

"I wasn't expecting it either," Juliet muttered. "I'm sorry you were worried. But I'm okay."

A total and utter lie. Her insides felt as if she'd sanded them with sharp, grainy silt and then swallowed seawater. She longed for the hollowness she'd carried for the past year. Nothingness was vastly preferable to *this*.

Juliet needed to call Elise immediately and tell her EA International's computer program was fundamentally flawed. She and Finn were not a good match, they weren't meant to be together and if Juliet never saw him again, it would be too soon.

Her mother held Juliet at arm's length, peering over her reading glasses to do a sweeping once-over of her daughter. "Where've you been? Elise said we shouldn't worry, but it was like you dropped off the face of the earth. Did something happen with Prince Alain?"

Finn had insisted it was okay to tell the truth about what had happened, as if he could have stopped her from blabbing to everyone what he'd done, but the righteous burn of anger had so drained her, now that she had the chance to flay him alive to her parents, she couldn't open her mouth.

She just wanted to be here in the circle of her family, where no one had hidden motives and everyone loved her. She wanted to forget, not feed the flames.

"It's a long story. Nothing happened with Finn. Nothing is going to happen with him. I'll tell you the rest some other time."

Collette, her youngest sister and the only Villere sibling still living at home, clasped her hands together with bright anticipation. "Will you be going back to America then, or are you staying here?"

"I'm here for now. I have no idea what my plans are."

"Oh." Collette's face fell. "I got permission to visit you in America. I was hoping you were going back."

Maybe Juliet shouldn't have been so forthcoming with her family about her plans to marry an American. Of course, when she'd left Delamer, she hadn't expected to be back home, heart shredded again courtesy of the Triple Blade Finn Special.

"We're happy you're home, and you may stay as long as you like," her father said gruffly, with a warning glare at Collette, and gave Juliet a one-armed hug. "We have to move fast now that the king's announced he's sending forces to join the other countries standing up against Alhendra."

That hadn't taken long. Finn had probably blown the "all hands on deck" horn the moment he hit the palace doors, firmly in his element.

Her father clapped his hands. "We're organizing a protest and you're our best strategist. It's a shame it didn't work with the prince. We could have used him on our side."

Juliet's legs weakened and she sank to the couch. She'd been home five minutes and they wanted to get started on another protest? Her parents were no better than Finn's.

"I'm pretty tired."

Did *everyone* want her around only for what she could do for them?

"Of course you are, dear. That's enough for now, Eduard." Her mother bustled Juliet into the kitchen to ply her with crepes stuffed with fruit and a steaming cup of Italian coffee. Their best. Because she was the prodigal daughter, returning to the fold after running away to America.

Her family loved her. They weren't glad she'd come home so they could channel her passion against the king or hijack her strategic mind. Finn's betrayal colored everything, but not everyone was like him, using people for his or her own agenda.

No one mentioned Alhendra or protests for the rest of the day, and Juliet's spine slowly became less rigid. But when she stopped bracing for the next round of gleeful hand-rubbing over how to best foil King Laurent, her mind wandered to Finn, and she could still smell him on her skin.

Just a few hours ago, they'd twined their limbs together so tightly, it was a wonder the scent of his arousal and excitement hadn't infused her blood.

Leaping up in the middle of Collette's impassioned speech about why she should get to go to university in America, Juliet fled upstairs to her parents' one narrow bathroom and took a tepid shower, the best the water heater could do. She scrubbed and scrubbed but the scent of well-loved man wouldn't vacate her nose.

She dried off and buried herself in the spare bed, quilts up to her neck. And that's when the tears flowed. Crying. Over a cretin whom she never should have trusted in the first place. Who had systematically broken down her defenses in a plot to discredit her family's position against the king.

But in her mind's eye, she could relive only the absolute relief she'd experienced when he'd pulled her from the water. The care and concern in his expression as he watched over her while she burned with fever. The glint in his eye when he confessed he was still in love with her.

All lies and manipulation. Had to be.

By morning, she'd slept only a few hours and developed a raging need to do something—anything—to wash Prince Alain from her system once and for all. And if it hurt him, so much the better.

She cornered her father in the kitchen. "Let's talk about that protest."

Over the next few days, Juliet routed her energy into managing her sisters, cousins, aunts, uncles, their various spouses and offspring, as well as her parents, into a protest machine of the first order. Even the littlest ones could color fliers or staple pamphlets, and she corralled everyone with a fervor that earned her the nickname General Juliet.

The irony of the military-influenced moniker she could do without.

An organized protest was her first goal and the king's head on a platter her second. Figuratively, of course, but if it happened for real in her dreams, no one else had to know.

If King Laurent would simply call the warships home and show a commitment to staying out of foreign conflicts, that would work too. Then they'd have a shot at softening the remaining military mandates. Finally.

The Villere household buzzed with activity toward that end from dawn until midnight, which Juliet embraced wholeheartedly because she never had time to think. She didn't have the luxury of counting the days until a pregnancy test might yield accurate results, thus determining the course of her future.

At night, she shared her bed with a cousin, sister or niece—sometimes more than one—and the cramped quarters suited her well. If she wasn't alone, she couldn't cry, but the tears were there, waiting for the right tipping point to spill out.

One afternoon, as Juliet argued via phone with the local magistrate about a permit to assemble, Gertrude tugged on her skirt and held up a plain brown paper-wrapped package, proudly clutched tight in her five-year-old hands.

Please be the missing four-color mailers. They'd gotten only half the order from the printer and they had little time to go back to press. The protest was scheduled for tomorrow, at the palace gates.

"Thank you," Juliet mouthed to her cousin's daughter and set the package on the counter, sandwiching the phone between her shoulder and ear to slice the neatly taped lid with kitchen shears. "I'm aware the normal processing time is five days, Mr. Le Clercq," she said into the phone. "I'm asking for an exception."

She flipped the box open. The phone dropped from her shoulder and clattered to the floor.

Shoes. The box contained shoes—*her* shoes. Alligator sandals lay nestled in carefully arranged padding. The same ones she'd worn on her dinner date with Finn, back in Dallas, which she'd donned with a hesitant sense of hope. The same ones she thought she'd lost when she woke up barefooted in the dark, with Finn's voice as her only guide.

The cuts had healed where she'd tramped barefoot across the rocky shore of Île de Etienne. But the internal scars she'd developed there…those she could never be rid of.

"Are you ill?" Aunt Vivian eyed her from across the room, her warm brown eyes magnified by thick glasses.

Juliet waved at her, too numb and speechless to respond.

How in the world had these come back to her? Mystified, she glanced at the return label she hadn't bothered to read because she'd assumed the contents would be something far more innocuous.

Finn. Her heart squeezed. He'd sent them. Which meant he'd had them all along. Something sharp knifed through her chest. If only he could return the rest of what he'd taken from her. The possibility of a different match with EA International. Her ability to trust. Her ability to forget, especially if she ended up pregnant after all.

And now this. A physical reminder of what she'd gambled and lost.

Hands shaking, she smashed the lid closed, covering the sandals, and stuffed the box in the back of the pantry in a place no one would find it. Then she put a sack of potatoes on top.

Unable to quite catch her breath, Juliet fled to the living room, where Uncle Jean-Louis was dozing in front of the lone TV. The simple Villere house sported few of the luxuries she'd experienced while staying in Alexander's house, but she'd take it ten times out of ten over anything else. Especially a residence with a Montagne in it.

She just needed a couple of minutes to get the threat of tears a bit more under control. It wouldn't do for anyone to know she was upset or that a mere man had so negatively affected her. Mindless entertainment would fix her up in a jiffy.

Predictably, the remote was nowhere to be found and the news channel her uncle had tuned to was covering the conglomeration of warships in the Mediterranean off the coast of Greece. Because that was *all* the news stations discussed, as well as her family, she knew Finn was on one. Good. That meant he'd taken her request to stay away from her to heart.

And that was the tipping point. A single tear broke loose, tracking down her cheek. Then another, and suddenly the floodgates busted from their moorings.

This was clearly the wrong place to decompress.

As she was about to stand and flee, Aunt Vivian popped her head into the room and shoved Juliet's phone at her. "Weren't you talking to someone—oh, *cherie*. What's wrong?"

Mortified, Juliet shook her head and motioned the elder woman to go back to the kitchen. There was no way she could speak coherently. Neither did she want to, not even to her favorite aunt.

Vivian ignored the clear "go away" sign and shuffled to the couch to engulf Juliet in a warm hug. "It's not as bad as all that, is it?"

Juliet pressed her face into her aunt's midsection and nodded, too beyond any sense of control to care that she'd wet Vivian's dress through. She was still in love with Finn and apparently nothing he did, no matter how much he hurt her, could erase it.

"Your young man is a fool," Vivian clucked. "You'd think royal DNA would produce more sense."

Juliet's neck jerked involuntarily and she glanced up at her aunt. Had her mother spilled all her daughter's recent activities to her sister? "How did you know I was crying over Finn?"

She smiled and nodded at the TV. "He's a handsome devil but clearly addled in the head if he's given you up."

Finn's handsome face indeed filled the screen as he answered a reporter's questions. Clad in his finest dress uniform decorated with medals of honor, he was breathtaking. Literally. Her lungs hitched and she meant to look away. But couldn't.

Greedily, she searched his face for any clue, no matter how small, to his state of mind. Did he miss her? Was he sorry? She hoped he lay awake at night and suffered. As she did.

Absently, she gnawed on a fingernail. When he smiled at the reporter, it wasn't the same one he always gave Juliet. Fine lines around his mouth and eyes crinkled, aging him. He looked worn out.

When would the urge to soothe him and make sure he took care of himself go away?

Aunt Vivian settled next to Juliet on the sofa, careful not to disturb Uncle Jean-Louis, though a freight train at full speed probably wouldn't wake him. Juliet glanced at her aunt, who seemed content to quietly watch the clip with her.

"The first round of negotiations went well," Finn said into the microphone.

Negotiations?

Warships had assembled in the Ionian Sea to intimidate Alhendra into meekly laying down its arms. Might made right after all, in the minds of those with the might. At what point did anyone ever intend to negotiate?

Finn continued speaking smoothly in his rich public address voice. His royal DNA might have left out any sense, but it certainly afforded him authoritative command under pressure and the ability to look devastating while doing it.

He wrapped up with, "I'm gratified to be a member of the contingent invited into the interior of Alhendra. We hope to have a peaceful cease-fire and an end to this standoff signed and delivered this afternoon."

Finn was a member of the diplomatic committee nego-tiating with Alhendra? Juliet shook her head, but the ban-ner scrolling across the bottom of the screen reiterated that point in capital letters. Not only was he a member of the committee, but Finn had been instrumental in getting through the ordeal with no discharge of weapons.

He wasn't a diplomat. He was far too pigheaded and obstinate. Wasn't he?

"What was the key to the negotiations?" the reporter asked.

"Meeting in the middle," Finn responded immediately, and the words seared through Juliet's stomach. The same thing he'd asked her to do, but then refused to budge from his side even one little centimeter.

Yet he'd done it successfully with an entire country. How?

The question stayed with her as she tossed fitfully that night. Fortunately, she'd had the foresight to bar any cous-ins or siblings from her room, citing a need for alone-time. Too much weighed on her mind to sleep. The protest was in the morning, and they'd be doing it illegally since she'd failed to secure the permit to assemble in time.

Juliet would probably be arrested again. At least this time she wasn't publicly linked with Finn, thus saving him the embarrassment of it.

And why would she care? He deserved everything she had to throw at him.

The sentiment rang false in the darkened room.

Regardless of how much Bernard's death had hurt her personally and hurt her family, Finn hadn't deserved the fallout from Juliet's role in the first protest. It had been a mistake. Born of highly charged emotions, sure, but han-dled very poorly, especially given that she'd claimed to be in love with him.

For the first time, she thought about how he must have felt. How he must have seen it as a betrayal and a clear division of sides. She'd chosen family over Finn. Kind of like what she'd accused him of doing back on Île de Etienne.

Her eyes burned with unshed tears. Finn had hurt her—but that didn't mean he didn't love her. Sometimes people messed up, and trying to forget about their mistakes wasn't the answer.

Her fingers felt for the knob of the bedside table, and she pulled open the drawer to extract the book inside, then snapped on the light. Each page contained a pressed flower, one from every bouquet Finn had given her. Why she'd kept it, tucked away here in her childhood home, escaped her.

Tonight, as she ran a fingertip over first one stalk, then the next, it comforted her. These blooms had once been alive, thriving, stretching toward the sun, and should by all rights have disintegrated into dust by now. It was the sad cycle of life for a flower. But she'd carefully preserved each one, pressing it dry until she had something that would last a very long time.

Was there something similar she should have done—but hadn't—to break the cycle she and Finn seemed destined to travel? All she knew was that she was miserable without him and wanted it to stop.

She clutched the book to her chest and held it until dawn. As the sun rose and light filtered through the curtains, warmth entered her body for the first time since she'd left Île de Etienne. And she was at peace with what came next.

They had to cancel the protest.

Finn had resolved the conflict by influencing everyone to compromise. She could compromise too. For real this time, by not leading a protest against the father of the man she loved. At least half—or maybe all—of her motivation in participating in the protest had more to do with their breakup. Not because she truly believed in the cause.

She'd started the cycle—it was up to her to end it. Her relationship with Finn might never recover from the stupid things they'd both done, but that could be dealt with later.

She had a protest to stop.

People milled through the kitchen, fired up and ready to see heads roll.

"The nerve," her father said, and stabbed a finger at the morning paper's headlines. "The palace is hosting a ball tonight to celebrate Delamer successfully throwing its weight around in Alhendra."

Her mother chimed in. "We're moving the protest to this evening. We'll stand arm to arm across the road by the gates and refuse to let anyone's limousine pass. It'll be very effective as all those wealthy, entitled people wait endlessly in their finery. They'll be forced to read our signs and hear our voices united against the king."

Juliet's sleep-deprived brain had difficulty keeping up with the rapid turn of the conversation. Those *wealthy, entitled people* were the friends and family of Finn, who had resolved what could have been a bloody mess without any loss of life.

"But the conflict is over. They said so on the news yesterday. What are you protesting?"

"It goes against everything we believe in." Her father thumped the table, rattling all the silverware and earning a murmured *here-here* from several of her relatives. "Romanticizing war and aggression with an expensive party and honoring those who traipsed off to perpetuate it is almost worse than forcing young boys into service."

"The king requires mandatory service because Delamer is such a small country," she blurted out. Her father stared at her as if she'd lost her mind, when in actuality, she'd just found it. "The armed forces would be a joke without it."

She'd heard Finn say it a dozen times. But never really listened. She touched the linked hearts fastened to the chain under her dress, one a mirror of the other. She and Finn were matched because they were exactly alike. Passionate. Stubborn. As often as she'd accused Finn of refusing to budge from his side, how many steps had she taken toward his?

He hadn't championed military reform to his father because he hadn't bought into it—and she'd completely discounted his reasons. He loved his people and loved his job. How much had she hurt him by refusing to see that was why he didn't take her side?

The hearts on her necklace clutched each other, one keeping the other from falling. But that worked only if the other reached back. Real love wasn't about what you had to give up but what you gained when you held on. That was Elise's message.

"Half the country borders water," Juliet continued. "Mandatory service leads to a strong naval presence. And maybe that's not the best way to staff the military, but we should be offering alternatives, not protests."

"Juliet!" Her mother's mouth pinched together, trembling. "Your brother died because of that philosophy."

"Bernard's death was an accident. We have to move on. Forgive ourselves and stop blaming the king. It's no one's fault. Which is the very definition of an accident."

The burden she'd carried for over a year lifted. Not completely, but enough. It wasn't her fault Bernard died. It wasn't the king's. It certainly wasn't Finn's, but she'd transferred some of her own guilt to him unconsciously. Guilt because she'd introduced Bernard and Finn. Guilt because she'd not better taught Bernard to listen when his superior officers listed safety regulations. That guilt had driven a lot of her decisions but no more.

She squared her shoulders. "The protest is illegal. We shouldn't do it for that reason alone. But maybe a protest isn't the best way to handle this in the first place. Let's try diplomacy for once."

"The way the king leads should be what's criminal, not a civilized protest. You had a chance to use diplomacy with the prince. That's why we're doing it this way." Her father swept her with his hard, cynical gaze, but she saw only a broken man who'd lost his son. It was easy to forgive him.

"You go ahead with the protest, if that's your choice. But you'll do it without me."

Juliet turned and left the room. She used Skype to contact Elise on the other side of the world, then realized it was still early morning in Dallas. Shockingly, the matchmaker answered almost immediately.

"Juliet. Is everything okay?" Elise had enabled video and Juliet could see her short, dark hair was slightly mussed, as if she'd rolled from bed.

"I was about to disconnect. Sorry to wake you."

"You didn't."

Oh. Elise wasn't alone and worse, had been dragged away from something much more fun than a surprise call. "*Really* sorry to disturb you then."

The matchmaker laughed, but the wistfulness in her expression wasn't hard to read. "I was neck-deep in my budget. I only wish I had a better reason to be awake this early."

In the month Juliet had lived with Elise during her makeover, the matchmaker hadn't dated at all. But she obviously wanted to meet someone and clearly loved a good happily-ever-after. Why didn't Elise enter her own information in EA International's computer and find herself a match? It would only make sense.

"Well, since you're awake, I need your help." Juliet bit her lip and went for broke. It took her ten minutes, but she told Elise the whole horrible story, including the part about her own failings.

It wasn't so easy to forgive herself, but she'd taken the first step. Now she had to take several more, and there was only one place adequate enough, public enough, to do it.

"What can I do?" Elise asked. "Name it and it's yours."

Juliet didn't hesitate. "Wave your fairy godmother wand and make me look like someone worthy of a prince. I'm going to the ball."

Thirteen

Finn's head ached. The limo hadn't moved in ten minutes, but that was okay. The faster it moved, the sooner he'd get to the palace and honestly, he wasn't sure how much more back-clapping and accolades and festivity he could handle.

The conflict with Alhendra was over. But the tension Finn had carried for days wasn't.

With only Gomez and LaSalle for company, Finn had visited the neighborhood in Preveza. Alhendra's missile had decimated twelve blocks, killing four hundred people and leveling buildings. The city would never be the same. It haunted him.

The carnage propelled him to insist on being a part of the diplomatic committee working with Alhendra to put an end to the standoff. His father should have been the one, or Alexander at the very least, but it spoke of Delamer's standing in the United Nations that no one batted an eye when King Laurent announced Finn would be the delegate for his country.

His father's faith in him meant everything. Enough to forgive the king for his role in the kidnapping.

That vivid imagery of the devastated bombing site stayed with him through the cease-fire negotiations. It fueled him, energized him to the point of crystalline determination—Alhendra's leaders would not walk out of that room without agreeing to turn over their weapons. Period. But neither would he allow his ships or anyone else's to fire on Alhendra in retaliation.

Compromise.

It had worked.

He'd intended only to resolve the conflict—and in the process, he'd used the opportunity to expand his role, his usefulness to the crown. He'd made it what he wanted it to be instead of waiting for someone to define it for him. No longer did he feel boxed in by his birth order or as if the military was all he had or could hope to have. The sky was the limit.

The victory was bittersweet because Juliet wasn't there to share it with him.

Finn peered out the limo's front window. The taillights of the town car in front of them flashed as the traffic screeched to a halt again. "What's going on, James?" Finn called to the driver.

"There are several people in the street," James said, eyes trained to the road ahead. "They appear to be blocking traffic."

That's what Finn got for going back to his modest house late last night after arriving in Delamer via plane, well ahead of the ships scheduled to return today. But he'd wanted to be alone and then his mother sprang this ball on him, insisting a party in his honor was the least she could do to show pride in her son. How could he say no?

"I'll walk from here, thanks." Finn reached for the door handle. "If you can get out of this snarl, go have a cup of coffee somewhere. I'll text you when I'm ready to leave."

He hit the pavement and Gomez and LaSalle followed. His bodyguards stayed glued to his side now that Finn had international celebrity for something other than the number of shots he could do in a row. Unfortunately, resolving a conflict with extremists solicited much more dangerous attention than that of paparazzi and socialites.

As Finn neared the palace gates, shouts from the people blocking traffic grew clearer.

Peace not war. No more warships.

The shouting people carried signs, holding them aloft and waving them at those trying to enter the palace gates.

It was a protest. Icy waves cut through Finn's stomach. Not this again, not now.

Almost against his will, he searched the faces, though it was almost unnecessary to confirm his suspicions about the identity of the protesters. But he had to know.

His eyes locked with Collette Villere. Juliet's sister.

The disappointment was sharp. But what had he expected? Of course Juliet was here with her family, standing on her side of the line with pride and stubborn determination. Nonetheless, something died inside, something he'd have sworn had been killed off long ago.

His gaze traveled down the row of Villere protesters but Juliet's brown hair and slight form wasn't among them. A ridiculous and fleeting bloom of hope unfurled. Ridiculous because she was probably perched halfway up one of the stone balustrades flanking the gates, bullhorn in hand, inciting the crowd verbally as her family held signs.

But she wasn't. Juliet was nowhere to be found.

Collette was too far away in the crush of people and vehicles to ask after Juliet's whereabouts. With one last puzzled glance over his shoulder, Finn walked the remaining five hundred yards up the paved entrance to the palace and mounted the steps.

Two footmen opened the wide oak doors, one to each side, and admitted him to the grand foyer. Finn paused at the head of the marble steps leading to the floor below, while another footman announced him, droning out his full title with pomp and ceremony. Necks craned as his name caught the attention of the crowd of partygoers below who had braved the walk to the palace from their boxed-in vehicles.

Applause broke out and Finn took it with a grin. What else could he do? These were his people and he'd walked into negotiations with Alhendra on their behalf. It was nice to know they appreciated his efforts.

Finn mingled with the crowd, accepting the hearty back-slaps and handshakes with as much cheer as he could muster, but his throat burned with each *bonsoir* and *how are you* he said. Unbelievably, no one wanted to discuss Alhendra, but the identity of the protesters outside was on everyone's lips. The sidelong glances and blatant comments about the year-old scandal from every knot of people Finn encountered grew tiresome.

Especially since both Alexander *and* his father got in on that action.

Thankfully, no one mentioned Juliet by name. Obviously she hadn't joined her family yet but the instant she did, placard in hand and shouts for justice raised above the noise of the street, he'd undoubtedly hear about it.

Alexander left to go home to the still-bedridden Portia, and King Laurent abandoned Finn to talk racehorses with his brother, the Duke of Carlier. As they'd competed against each other on the track for over forty years, Finn could have repeated their conversation verbatim without hearing a syllable of it. He was glad to be alone for a moment.

The queen worked her way over to Finn, and he bussed both cheeks. "You look stunning, Mother. This is a great party."

"Go on." She swiped at Finn with a gloved hand, but the tenderness she'd always held for her youngest shone from her eyes. "I'm glad you're home safe. I sent some of the grounds crew to the gates to deal with that...issue. Hopefully they won't disturb us further."

A shadow leached the pleasure from the queen's face.

When would this ever end? Juliet and her family were ruining his mother's party.

Finn excused himself as the Earl of Ghent struck up a conversation with his mother and scouted in vain for a passing tray of champagne. What kind of party was this where the hostess tortured her son with invisible waitstaff?

Finally, he caught up with a beleaguered waiter on the far side of the hall. The crush was stifling; more than a hundred and fifty people milled and laughed and celebrated. Normally Finn loved a good party, but this was overwhelming.

He raised the flute of champagne to his lips as a murmur broke out over the crowd, their gazes cutting toward the entrance. A footman called out, "Miss Juliet Villere."

The name echoed over and over and faded away until dead silence cloaked the room. Then, there she was.

Juliet paused at the head of the stairs, and the flute nearly slipped from Finn's suddenly numb fingers. She was resplendent in a shimmery gown, so light and airy, it looked as if it had been spun from a hundred silver spiders. Fit only for a princess. Hair swept up and pinned, face accented with a hint of color, she stole his breath.

What was she doing here?

She was pregnant. Joy flooded him so fast, his knees turned to jelly.

No, it was too soon to know that. There was only one reason she'd crashed the ball.

His stomach twisting with tension, Finn started toward her, fully intending to personally throw her out on her admittedly spectacular rear end. How dare she waltz in here? If she thought she was going to bring her rabble-rousing, anti-military rants into his mother's party, she had more nerve and less intelligence than he'd ever credited.

Juliet Villere was not going to embarrass or upset his mother.

The crowd parted as he marched through. More than a hundred feet separated him from Juliet, but their gazes locked and something gentle and shiny welled in hers.

"Stop!" she commanded, the word reverberating in the quiet hall.

Finn was so surprised, he did.

"Wait there." Juliet gathered her skirt in one hand and descended the stairs slowly, with a grace he'd never seen. She moved like an apparition, like a vision. Was that what was going on? He'd fallen asleep and dreamed up this scene?

Juliet reached the floor, flanked by wide-eyed guests in beaded gowns and black tie. She watched him as she approached, her gaze steady and unapologetic.

Everything broken inside ached that he couldn't greet her as a lover, with a passionate kiss. That they'd parted with insurmountable differences separating them.

"What do you want?" he called harshly.

Her smile was shaky but for him alone. "For you to stand there while I cross this huge expanse of middle ground."

His eyelids shut and he swallowed, but the tightness in his throat wouldn't ease. When he opened his eyes, she was still moving toward him, beautiful and real and exactly what he'd always wanted. She wasn't compromising—this was something far more profound.

She'd come here to try again, not to embarrass him or bring the protest inside. She wasn't even participating in the protest. She was siding with Finn, not her family. Publicly. It was an apology for participating in the first protest, the very antithesis of what she'd done a year ago.

Something massive welled up and broke over him in a wave, healing so many of his deep wounds instantly.

But then she stopped just past the halfway point. She

glanced down and then back up, her expression clouded. The message was clear.

She wanted him to meet her in the middle.

After her brave entrance to this ball, uninvited and unwelcome, how could he not?

Yet he hesitated, the man and the prince at war, as always.

Juliet's dramatic and public move meant a lot to him. But what had really changed between them? They would be right back in the same boat next week—battling out their opposite agendas and being stubborn and holding grudges. Their families would always be a problem, always interfere with their relationship.

He couldn't do this again, this back-and-forth dance between the duty and privilege of his title and the simple life he wished for where he was just a man who loved a woman.

He couldn't walk across that middle ground.

So Finn sank to his knees and crawled to the woman he loved.

Juliet nearly dissolved into a big puddle of sensations as Finn crossed the remaining expanse of marble on his hands and knees.

The murmurs of the crowd melted away as he reached her and rose up on his knees to take her hand. His beautiful eyes sought hers and out poured the contents of his soul.

"What are you doing?" she asked, emotion clogging her throat.

"I didn't have any broken glass to crawl over. But I'm here to tell you marble is a close second in the pain department," he said wryly with an endearing wince.

"But why are you crawling at all? Here, in front of everyone." The curious crowd pressed in, anxious to catch every word of the drama unfolding around them in all its titillating splendor.

"We can't keep going through the same endless loop,

arguing and hurting each other. It has to be different this time. You did your half, wanting me to meet you in the middle. So I did."

Oh, goodness. Her heart tripped once and settled back in her chest, content and peaceful for the first time in… forever.

He was coming to her as a man, not a prince.

It was symbolic—and so unnecessary. She shook her head. "I'm the one who needed to take those steps. You're who you are by blood, and I selfishly tried to stand in the way of that. Testing you to see if I was more important than your heritage, demanding proof of your devotion by asking you to be someone ordinary. I don't want that. Stand up. I want Prince Alain in all his glory."

Prince, lieutenant, helicopter pilot, lover, friend, rescuer and occasional video game partner—all rolled into one delicious package.

The crowd gasped and tittered and a couple of the women clapped. One was the queen. That seemed like a plus in Juliet's favor.

Still clasping her hand, Finn climbed to his feet, his expression solemn as he called out to the room at large. "Show's over, folks. Go back to the party and enjoy my mother's incredible hospitality."

Dispersing with glacial speed, the crowd drifted back to their conversations and champagne, shooed away largely by the queen herself. Juliet could really learn to like Finn's mother.

To Juliet, Finn simply said, "Dance with me."

Oh, no. Now she had to come clean.

"Is this the part where I should admit the buckle on my shoe broke?" Her mouth twitched and she tried really hard to keep the laugh from bubbling out. "I can't exactly walk."

She stuck her foot out from under the gossamer skirt to show him the offending alligator sandals that she'd rescued from beneath the potatoes. That had probably been the last straw for these poor shoes, which had followed her through thick and thin as she figured out the most important lessons of her life. There was no way she'd have worn any other pair tonight.

"*That's* why you stopped?" A hundred emotions vied for purchase on his face, and he finally picked self-deprecating amusement. "You were going to cross the entire length of the floor, weren't you?"

She nodded. "It was the least you deserved. I'm sorry I was so shortsighted over the last year. And I'm sorry for the protest. It was wrong and I shouldn't have done it. I love you. And did very little to show you how much."

A wealth of emotion swept over his face in a tide, transforming him from merely handsome to magnificent.

"I made mistakes too." He drew her hand to his mouth and pressed his lips to the back of her hand in a long kiss. "My blood may be blue but the organ pumping it belongs to you. Not my father, not Delamer. I love you too, more than I love anything. I'm sorry I didn't honor my relationship with you above them."

The words were sweet and the thrill in her chest even sweeter. That's what made it easy to refute his mixed-up declaration.

"But I'm saying I don't want you to choose me above them any longer. That was our problem all along. Too much pressure to make choices between absolutes. Love obviously isn't enough. Let's find the middle ground."

He grinned. "I take it you liked my speech. I had no idea it would produce all this." He motioned to her dress. "You're the most gorgeous woman here."

A blush that she hoped was becoming fired up in her cheeks.

"It was inspiring. But I think my fairy godmother had more to do with this look than anything. Elise," she clarified when he raised his brows. "You don't think I put this outfit together by myself, do you?"

The benefits of Skype and a webcam for the consummate tomboy could not be overstated. Elise deserved a bonus for working her magic across fiber-optic lines.

"I'm more interested in what's under it than how it came to be."

Heat zigzagged between them and her abdomen fluttered. "What's under it is a woman who's lousy at forgetting the past. Let's try forgiveness instead, shall we? Please, please forgive me for all the horrible hurt I've caused you."

So easy. The answer had been there all along. Forgiveness was the key, not forgetting.

Eyes shiny with tenderness, he smiled. "Already done. Will you do the same for me?"

"Done." She returned the smile and bumped his knee with hers. "That happened the moment you hit the marble. Are we going to make it this time, then?"

"Yes." He nodded decisively. "I couldn't possibly let you get away again. You're going to have to marry me. No pregnancy required, though I'd welcome one at some point in the future."

Princess Juliet. The thought shivered down her spine with equal parts trepidation and awe. "Is this a marriage proposal?"

He shook his head. "More of a promise of one to come, when I'm not so unprepared and dazzled by your sheer beauty." But then he paused and his expression turned earnest. "You'd be a princess for life. A card-carrying member of the House of Couronne. Princess Juliet of Montagne, Duchess of Marechal, along with a ton of other unwieldy titles. Can you do it?"

He didn't mean just the jumble of new names and royal protocol. She'd be choosing him over her family, over her commoner heritage, over Bernard's memory. She'd be far past that middle ground every day, forever. Thank goodness.

Best of all, Elise's efforts toward polishing Juliet's rough edges would actually pay off.

Her grip on his hand tightened. "The better question is, can you? I'm not diplomatic like you. I have opinions and I'll not be shy in giving them to you. The people may never forgive you for marrying me."

"They will. Because they'll see what I see. The People's Princess, who believes passionately in their best interests. You got that new school built. You care about their lives or you wouldn't have protested the mandatory service law."

In his eyes, all the qualities he'd listed reflected back at her. Elise's computer had matched them because they shared a bone-deep belief in their convictions. They were a passionate, stubborn, yet thoroughly formidable team, and together they could change the world.

"Besides," he continued, "when I came across the floor on my knees, it was as public of a declaration as yours. I'm on your side. Everyone will know that by the time the sun rises tomorrow."

"And I'm on your side." The best compromise—instead of giving a little, they'd both gained everything.

He drew her into his arms and said the sweetest words of all. "Let's get out of here."

She smiled, tipping her face up to bask in his potent, wonderful masculine strength. "That's the best royal decree I've ever heard."

She started to follow him and her alligator sandal fell off, broken buckle clattering to the marble. Before her Prince Charming could escape, she thumbed off the other one and left them both in the middle of the ball.

Where she hoped Finn was taking her—straight to heaven—shoes were optional.

Epilogue

Finn slid the patio door open with his hip and stepped out, champagne in one hand and flutes in the other. Île de Etienne spread out around him, its beauty unchanged in the month since he'd left it via helicopter, crushed and hopeless. Head tipped back, Juliet lay on the cushion lining the wooden patio chair they'd selected to replace the ones sacrificed to fire on the rocky shore below them.

She popped an eye open. "I thought you were taking a call. This looks like a celebration."

"It is." He poured her a glass and then filled his, dinging the rims together lightly. "Alexander just texted me. The papers are processed. Île de Etienne belongs to us."

"Well, technically just you," she corrected as he sat on the next chaise lounge. "Your father's horribly outdated laws don't allow us to own property jointly unless we're married."

"About that," he began casually and toyed with the stem of his flute to cover a sudden bout of the shakes.

Nerves? Really? He'd faced down an extremist government without blinking yet freaked out over a little overt display of affection for a woman who deserved the moon.

Their rocky relationship had finally smoothed out. The past could never be forgotten until it was forgiven, and once that happened, they both lost the desire to prove the other wrong or take sides. It made all the difference.

He cleared his throat and nodded toward the west. "You might want to glance in that direction."

She did and gasped. Written across the breathtaking blue expanse of sky were the words *MARRY ME JULIET* in white smoke. His version of an outrageously romantic proposal. Hopefully she'd think so too.

"A skywriter?" She shot him a glance full of her own brand of overt affection. "Is he on call to also post my response for the whole of Delamer to witness?"

Finn grinned. In one small sentence, she'd put them back on comfortable ground. "If you like. We're going to be in the public eye for a long time. Might as well give them their money's worth."

"Do you have to pay by the letter?" Tapping her chin, she pretended to contemplate. "Because a 'no' would certainly be cheaper."

"Not considering how much this set me back." He extended his hand to offer her his heart encased in gold. The ring was a simple band channel set with sapphires, but it was also one of the original Delamer crown jewels, circa the seventeenth century.

"Oh, Finn." Tears welled in her beautiful green eyes as she stared at the ring. "That's not expensive, it's priceless."

"You better believe it. I had to promise my mother you'd give her a grandchild within the year before she'd agree to let this out of the treasury." He held out his other hand, palm up, and she laid her hand in his without hesitation.

His Juliet was brave, bold and loved everything fiercely, especially him. He prayed he could spend the rest of his life returning it tenfold. "You're my calm in the storm and I need you. Will you marry me?"

She blinked back the still-present tears. "Are you sure? I'm not going to give up on convincing your father to pass the law giving kids a choice between mandatory military service and an internship for their eventual career."

The chuckle escaped before he could catch it. The next fifty years promised to be full of arguments and lots of really great makeup sex. "I don't want you to give up. How's this instead? Eighteen months of service and eighteen months of internship, if they want that instead of continued service."

The idea had come to him the instant she'd pleaded her case the night before. Internship allowed the next generation to begin learning their trade much faster, which in turn kept Delamer relevant and able to compete in the expanding global marketplace. The armed forces would continue to be staffed in the meantime.

"Compromise." Her smile lit her from within. "I like it."

He shrugged. "I've tried to tell you what a great team we are. Now, are you going to marry me or will I wither and die waiting around for you to decide?"

"I'll marry you." She squeezed his hand and he felt it clear to his toes. "But only if you promise I'll have the keys to your heart forever."

Something bright flared in his soul. "I'm afraid I don't have much choice in that. You've had them since the first moment I laid eyes on you right over there." He nodded at the shores of Delamer across the wide expanse of the Mediterranean. There, he was a prince. Here on Île de Etienne, with Juliet, he was just a man who loved a woman. The best of both worlds.

"Good. That means I can come in whenever I want and love you exactly as you deserve."

Finn slid the ring on her finger and kissed her to seal the start of their happily-ever-after.

* * * * *

Don't miss any of the
HAPPILY EVER AFTER INC. *trilogy*
from Kat Cantrell:

MATCHED TO A BILLIONAIRE
MATCHED TO A PRINCE
Available now

and

MATCHED TO HER RIVAL
Available September 2014

COMING NEXT MONTH FROM

H HARLEQUIN®

Desire

Available September 2, 2014

#2323 A TEXAN IN HER BED
Lone Star Legends • by Sara Orwig
When Texas billionaire Wyatt Milan learns that stunning TV personality Destiny Jones intends to stir up a century-long family feud, his plan to stop her leads to a seduction that threatens his guarded heart.

#2324 REUNITED WITH THE LASSITER BRIDE
Dynasties: The Lassiters • by Barbara Dunlop
Angelica Lassiter thought she'd lost Evan forever after her grandfather's will wrecked their engagement. But when their best friends' wedding forces them to walk down the aisle—as best man and maid of honor—sparks fly!

#2325 SINGLE MAN MEETS SINGLE MOM
Billionaires and Babies • by Jules Bennett
When Hollywood agent Ian is stranded with single mom Cassie, their desire spirals out of control. But to be the man and father Cassie and her daughter need, Ian will have to face his dark past.

#2326 HEIR TO SCANDAL
Secrets of Eden • by Andrea Laurence
When congressman Xander Langston returns home, he wants a second chance with his high school sweetheart, Rose. But will the secrets they're keeping—including the truth about Rose's ten-year-old son—ruin everything?

#2327 MATCHED TO HER RIVAL
Happily Ever After, Inc. • by Kat Cantrell
To prove to cynical media mogul Dax that she's no fraud, matchmaker Elise challenges him to become a client. Except her supposedly infallible match software spits out *her* name as his perfect match!

#2328 NOT THE BOSS'S BABY
The Beaumont Heirs • by Sarah M. Anderson
Chadwick Beaumont is tired of doing what everyone wants him to do. It's time he did what he wants. And he wants his secretary, Serena Chase—pregnant or not!

———————

REQUEST YOUR FREE BOOKS!
2 FREE NOVELS PLUS 2 FREE GIFTS!

ALWAYS POWERFUL, PASSIONATE AND PROVOCATIVE

YES! Please send me 2 FREE Harlequin Desire® novels and my 2 FREE gifts (gifts are worth about $10). After receiving them, if I don't wish to receive any more books, I can return the shipping statement marked "cancel." If I don't cancel, I will receive 6 brand-new novels every month and be billed just $4.55 per book in the U.S. or $4.99 per book in Canada. That's a savings of at least 13% off the cover price! It's quite a bargain! Shipping and handling is just 50¢ per book in the U.S. and 75¢ per book in Canada.* I understand that accepting the 2 free books and gifts places me under no obligation to buy anything. I can always return a shipment and cancel at any time. Even if I never buy another book, the two free books and gifts are mine to keep forever.

225/326 HDN F4ZC

Name	(PLEASE PRINT)	
Address		Apt. #
City	State/Prov.	Zip/Postal Code

Signature (if under 18, a parent or guardian must sign)

Mail to the **Harlequin® Reader Service:**
IN U.S.A.: P.O. Box 1867, Buffalo, NY 14240-1867
IN CANADA: P.O. Box 609, Fort Erie, Ontario L2A 5X3

Want to try two free books from another line?
Call 1-800-873-8635 or visit www.ReaderService.com.

* Terms and prices subject to change without notice. Prices do not include applicable taxes. Sales tax applicable in N.Y. Canadian residents will be charged applicable taxes. Offer not valid in Quebec. This offer is limited to one order per household. Not valid for current subscribers to Harlequin Desire books. All orders subject to credit approval. Credit or debit balances in a customer's account(s) may be offset by any other outstanding balance owed by or to the customer. Please allow 4 to 6 weeks for delivery. Offer available while quantities last.

Your Privacy—The Harlequin® Reader Service is committed to protecting your privacy. Our Privacy Policy is available online at www.ReaderService.com or upon request from the Harlequin Reader Service.

We make a portion of our mailing list available to reputable third parties that offer products we believe may interest you. If you prefer that we not exchange your name with third parties, or if you wish to clarify or modify your communication preferences, please visit us at www.ReaderService.com/consumerschoice or write to us at Harlequin Reader Service Preference Service, P.O. Box 9062, Buffalo, NY 14269. Include your complete name and address.

HD13R

"**I** shudder to think how far you'd go to get what you wanted."

His expression tightened. "Yeah? Well, we both know how far you'll go, don't we?"

It was a cutting blow. When her father's will left control of Lassiter Media to Evan, it had resulted in an all-out battle between the two of them. Even now, when they both knew it had been a test of her loyalty, their spirits were battered and bruised, their relationship shattered beyond repair.

"I thought I was protecting my family," she defended.

At the time, she couldn't come up with any explanation except that her father had lost his mind, or that Evan had brazenly manipulated J.D. into leaving him control of Lassiter Media.

"You figured you were right and everyone else was wrong?" His steps toward her appeared automatic. "You slept in my arms, told me you loved me, and then accused me of defrauding you out of nearly a billion dollars."

All the pieces had added up in her mind, and they had been damning for Evan. "Seducing me would have been an essential part of your overall plan to steal Lassiter Media."

"Shows you how little you know about me."

"I guess it does."

Even though she was agreeing, the answer seemed to anger him.

"You *should* have known me. You should have trusted me. My nefarious plan was all inside your suspicious little head. I never made it, never mind executed it."

"I had no way of knowing that at the time."

"You could have trusted me. That's what wives do with their husbands."

"We never got married."

"Your decision, not mine."

They stared at each other for a long moment.

"What do you want me to do?" she finally asked, then quickly added, "About Kayla and Matt's wedding?"

"Don't worry. I know you'd never ask what I wanted you to do about us."

His words brought a pain to Angelica's stomach. He was up there on his pedestal of self-righteous anger, and she was down here…missing him.

Don't miss
REUNITED WITH THE LASSITER BRIDE
by Barbara Dunlop.

Available September 2014 wherever
Harlequin® Desire books and ebooks are sold.